"...Like no fire we've seen before."

Loper wiped the sweat off his face. "I'm sending Sally May and the kids to town. They'll have to go the back way in case the highway is closed. I'll take my pickup and open pasture gates on the way out, so the cattle can drift."

"I'll start filling the spray rig with water."

Loper looked him straight in the eye and shook his head. "Forget the spray rig. This is like no fire we've seen before. It's a killer. Deputy Kile said, 'Drop everything and run like a rabbit.'"

"And with that advice, you're going to open pasture gates. Most rabbits don't do that."

"I'm the guy who signed the note at the bank, but don't worry, I'm getting out of here too." He looked off to the west. "Look at that smoke cloud!"

The Case of the Monster Fire

John R. Erickson

Illustrations by Gerald L. Holmes

Maverick Books, Inc.

MAVERICK BOOKS, INC.
Published by Maverick Books, Inc.
P.O. Box 549, Perryton, TX 79070
Phone: 806.435.7611
www.hankthecowdog.com

First published in the United States of America by Maverick Books, Inc. 2018.

1 3 5 7 9 10 8 6 4 2

Copyright © John R. Erickson, 2018

All rights reserved

LIBRARY OF CONGRESS CONTROL NUMBER: 2018932816

978-1-59188-171-1 (paperback); 978-1-59188-271-8 (hardcover)

Hank the Cowdog® is a registered trademark of John R. Erickson.

Printed in the United States of America

Dedicated to the hundreds of kind people who helped us after the wildfire of 2017, with special thanks to Scot and Tina Erickson, Mark Erickson, and George and Karen Chapman.

CONTENTS

CHAPTER ONE

The Mouse Didn't Run Down the Clock

It's me again, Hank the Cowdog. The main part of this story takes place in March, oh what a terrible day, but to get there, we have to go back to October. Around here, October always happens before March. I don't know why, it just does.

So it was October before the next March. Drover and I had spent the night at Slim's place, as we often do because, well, he lets us stay inside the house. I had been up for hours, going over a stalk of poperwick...a stack of pickerwarp on my disk, when I hicked a honk in the frizzling fubble.

Huh?

Sorry, I'm having a little trouble with my words. Every once in a while, we have this pablum, so bee sting beside the honey hive and the mouse ran down the clock. When that hurples, we murple the purple.

Huh?

Sorry, my attention drifted there for a second, but I'm back up to speed now. We were discussing the mouse problem. These mice keep running down our clocks, don't you see, and when the clocks run down, we don't know whether it's raining or Tuesday. Tuesdays are very important in the overall scheme of things, because without Tuesday, we would never be able to measure our rainfall.

Yawn.

You know, some of this isn't making sense. How did we get onto the subject of mice and clocks and Tuesday? I mean, what is Tuesday to a mouse?

Does anyone remember what we were talking about?

Wait, here we go. Early morning, and I mean EARLY. Dawn. First light. At that hour, most of your ordinary mutts are still sprawled out on the floor, pumping out a line of Z's. In other words, sleeping their lives away.

Not me, fellers. I take pride in being the first one up. In the Security Business, we have little time for sleeping. At first light, I'm on the jib of the jab...I'm on the job.

May I whisper a little secret? See, one of my greatest fears in life is being infected with the Slacker Virus. Drover's had it all his life, and we're talking about BAD, and I'm scared I might catch it.

That's why, every morning before daylight, I leap out of bed and start doing pushups and pull-ups...pretzels and pork rinds, ketchup on poperwick, and plan out my whole day's snizzle, whilst all the slackers of the world are still snickerdoodling.

Wait. I seem to have lost my choo-choo...my train of thought, that is, so let's take a deep breath and start all over.

Okay, Drover and I must have spent the night at Slim's place, now we're cookin', and I had been up for hours, grinding out reports and studying mops and chops...maps and charts, that is, while chained to my desk. I heard an odd sound... several odd sounds and cranked open one eye.

Wait, that can't be right. I'd been working for hours, so both eyes must have been open, yes, wide open, so if you don't mind, get a red pencil and mark out that business about "cranked open one eye." I was misquibbled...misquoted, shall we say.

3

Go ahead and mark it out. Thanks.

I heard a sound, looked up from my work, and saw...hang on, this is scary...I saw what appeared to be an Egyptian mummy creeping down the dark hallway, sliding its hand along the wall. Somehow radar hadn't picked him up. Well, you know me. When a mummy shows up in the house, we sound General Quackers.

General Quarters, it should be.

A strip of hair shot up along my backbone and a growl came rumbling up from the engine room. Fellers, I BARKED!

"Hush!"

Huh?

Did you hear that? The mummy said...wait a second. Do you suppose...ha ha. Okay, we can call off the alert. Everybody relax. Ha ha. No big deal, just a simple...hey, when radar doesn't pick 'em up, how are we supposed to know?

It was Slim Chance, but believe me, he looked like some kind of mummy monster, I mean pale face and puffy red eyes and a rat's nest of hair. And he was wearing boxer shorts too. That's on our Check List For Mummies. They almost always show up wearing boxer shorts.

Okay, things were starting to fall into place. The Elite Troops of the ranch's Security Division

had camped at Slim's place, and it was morning. It was also October and every dog on the force was exhausted.

Let me emphasize the *exhausted* part. See, if

portions of the preceding so-forth sounded, well, disjointed, that's why. Our team had been pushed to the limits of Doggie Endurance, I mean, eighteen-hour days, no breaks, no weekends or holidays, no time off, just the grinding routine of running the ranch.

So, yes, Drover and I had spent the night down at Slim's place, and I'm going to stand before you right now and admit that I might have dozed off at my desk—not a deep sleep, nothing like Drover, I mean, the runt was in a coma, but maybe I'd been drifting in and out of focus.

Hey, it happens, even to the Head of Ranch Security, but now I was wide awake and back on the job.

Slim had pried himself out of bed, and I watched as he stumbled into the kitchen and made himself some coffee. As usual, he turned on the stove burner and left the gas running whilst he scratched a wooden match across the matchbox. As usual, it took several scratches to light the match, so when he finally put it under the pan of water, we had a little propane explosion.

As usual, he seemed surprised. Duh. I mean, propane blows up when you leave it running. There are no exceptions. It happens every time, and the longer you dawdle, the bigger the pow.

If you wonder why cowboys don't have hair on the back of their hands, this is the reason. Slim has even lost eyebrows.

Incredible.

Dogs don't enjoy explosions in the morning. We would like to help our people when they don't function well, but do they ever listen to their dogs or ask for our advice? No. So we go through this every day of the world.

He finally got the water boiling and dumped some coffee into the pan. He waited a few minutes, then sloshed it into a cup. He hadn't washed that cup in two years, by the way, and it was exactly the color of two-year old coffee.

After downing a couple of slurps, he crept out on the porch in his drawers and a T-shirt and brought in an armload of firewood. Stepping over me and Drover...stepping over Stubtail, who was sprawled out on the floor, he picked his way across the room toward the...

"Hank, move!"

...picked his way across the room to the stove, tripping on Drover in the process. He opened the stove door and placed a strip of dry cedar bark on the coals, blew on the coals until the bark caught fire, and added a few sticks of hackberry. Before long, he had a nice little fire going, closed the door, and set the damper.

Then he glared down at us and grumbled, "If this outfit depended on y'all to build a fire, we'd freeze to death."

Oh brother. I ignored him.

You know, it's strange that our story should start with a fire, because that's how it's going to... no, that's all I can say. I mean, it was such an awful...

We can't talk about it, sorry, and don't beg or whine. I have to be firm on this. You know how I am about the children. Some parts of this job are just too scary for the little guys, and there's no fire insurance for spectators. I mean, what if your book bursted into flames?

Don't laugh. It could happen.

I'm not at liberty to reveal any more information because it's highly classified and you're not supposed to know any of this, so the next big question is...do you want to go on with the story?

If not, brush your teeth and go to bed. If you're still with me, thanks. This is going to be a toughie.

Where were we? Oh yes, Sally May's rotten little cat. He drives me batty, and he knows that he drives me batty. He thrives on driving me batty. It seems to be the whole purpose of his life. He went to kitty college and got a degree in Batty Driving, but one of these days...

We weren't talking about the cat.

Tell you what, let's take a little break and change chapters. If you don't show up for Chapter Two, I'll have to go on without you.

A Robot on
the Porch!

kay, I had been up most of the night working
on reports. Drover was sprawled across the
floor like spilled milk, sleeping his life away. Slim
had managed to build a cup of coffee without
blowing up the kitchen and had chunked up the
fire in the wood stove, and now he was sitting in
his big easy chair, like a king in his castle, with a
loyal dog at his feet. But then...

Suddenly Earoscanners began picking up
something outside the house. I made adjustments
on the antennas until we were getting a clear
signal. Data Control chewed on that and sent the
alert:

*"Tires on gravel, possible intrusion of
unidentified vehicle, activate Warning System*

and prepare to launch!"

We don't get much time to respond to these Morning Intrusions, and we never know who it might be. It doesn't matter. We have to give a professional response, ready or not, and that's what I did. The instant DC's message flashed across the screen, I went into Stage One Barking. It's wired into the system, don't you see. It's automatic, and loud.

WOOF!

Slim had just taken a slurp of coffee, and my woof goosed him so much, he spilled hot coffee on his shirt, shorts, and naked legs.

"Ow! Moron!" He flew out of the chair, spilling more coffee on the threadbare carpet, and glared at me like...I don't know what, and screeched, "What's wrong with you!"

What was wrong with me was that I was a highly-trained professional cowdog in charge of First Response Security. An unidentified vehicle had just entered our airspace. We'd picked it up on Earoscanners and were tracking its every movement. Data Control had sent down a Stage One Alert and was assembling the Firing Data.

That's what was wrong with me.

"Meathead! You scalded my legs!"

Oh brother. I didn't scald his legs. He scalded

his own skinny legs with his own coffee, and if he'd been wearing pants instead of sitting around half-naked, he wouldn't have scalded anything.

Oh, and did we have time for this silly discussion? An intruder, possibly an enemy agent, was creeping up on the house!

I can't be blamed for the lack of discipline on this ranch. We should have been scrambling jets and launching dogs. We should have been into Stage Two or Stage Three Barking. We should have been doing SOMETHING to defend his house and my ranch from Enemy Intrudement. Instead, he was yelling at the Head of Security and calling him a meathead.

In many ways, this is a lousy job. They don't pay us enough to put up with this. Oh well.

So there we were, carrying on a silly conversation in the midst of a crisis, but things kind of took care of themselves. By that time, Slim could hear the sound of tires crunching gravel outside. His eyes grew wide and he muttered, "Good honk, somebody just pulled up!"

Duh.

He rushed to the front window and peeked through the dusty, barf-colored curtains that had been there since the Civil War. "Oh great!"

Apparently it wasn't good news, because he was transformed into some kind of wild man. Maybe he didn't want to fight the intruder in his undershorts.

Wait, that doesn't sound right. I didn't mean to say that the intruder was showing up in his undershorts. That would be ridiculous. Intruders don't do that. I meant to say that Slim...let's just skip it.

As we've discussed before, Slim is usually not a ball of flames first thing in the morning. Sometimes we need to check his pulse to be sure he isn't a corpse. Remember that only minutes before, I had mistaken him for a mummy.

Give him two cups of coffee and thirty minutes of solitude, staring at flies on the wall, and he'll come around, but this deal had wrecked his train. He became an explosion of arms, legs, and desperate expressions.

He made a dash down the dark hallway and vanished into his bedroom. There, he tripped over the boots he'd left in the middle of the floor. I didn't see this with my own eyes but heard it, and knew the story: He never puts a boot into the closet if he can leave it in the middle of the floor.

Then I heard him say, "What in the cat hair is that old man doing over here at this hour of the morning?"

Who?

Bam Bam Bam!

Yipes, somebody was banging on the door! Well, we'd gotten an Alert from DC and our procedures were very clear: Make no assumptions about intruders until we see some ID and clear them through Security. As far as I was concerned, we had come under attack.

I went straight into Sirens and Lights. "On your feet, Drover, battle stations, Red Alert, we've got Charlies on the porch!"

You know, I get a kick out of waking him up. Hee hee. I mean, he started running before he got his eyes open, before his feet even hit the floor, and all four legs were pumping air.

"Help, murder, mayday, Charlies on the porch!"

"On your feet, soldier, and load up Number Three Warning Barks!"

He finally scrambled to his feet, got traction, and ran smooth into the coffee table. Down he went. "Help, they got me! Dog down! Oh my leg!"

There was more banging on the door, then a booming voice. "Slim? You in there?"

That raised the hair along my backbone, I mean, no more laughing at Stubtail. We're talking about a deep, snickister voice that didn't even sound human!

"Drover, the Charlies must have sent some kind of robot probe to break down the door!"

"Help!"

"The only thing between us and destruction is

us!"

"Help!"

"Take weapons and ammo and three of your best men, and crawl to the door!"

"I don't have three men."

"Perfect. You'll be harder to see."

"Yeah, but..."

"Move out and set up a firing position."

"Yeah, but..."

"If they bust through the door, let 'em have it, give 'em the full load. Any questions?"

"This leg's killing me!"

"That's not a question and nobody cares. On your feet, let's get this job done and go home."

"Can we go home first?"

"Negatory. Boots on the floor!"

"Hank, you might have to help me up. This old leg's really giving me fits."

Oh brother. "Okay, stand by for Assisted Lift." Using my nose and enormous neck muscles as a prying device, I managed to get his front end off the floor, then went to work lifting his bohunkus. "Okay, trooper, that's four on the floor. Get out there and unload some ordinance!"

"How 'bout you?"

"Fine, thanks. Go git 'em!"

He took two steps toward the door, stopped,

glanced back at me, and...you won't believe this. Drover is such a little chicken liver! I shouldn't have been surprised, but I was.

You know, my biggest problem in this job is that I'm a foolish optimist. I keep hoping to see progress in the men, a little sign that says I'm not wasting my life. I place too much faith in my fellow dogs and my heart gets broken every day. I keep hoping I can turn their lives around, but they keep turning *mine* around and upside-down and backwards.

I should have known he would weenie out of this mission. Do you know why? Because he'd done it a thousand times before, that's why.

Okay, let's get this sad situation out of the way. The King of Slackers marched two steps toward his combat assignment, cut a hard right turn, and went streaking down the hall to Slim's bedroom, where he vanished. I didn't see him slither under the bed, but I knew he did.

This was so predictable and so sad. You give your men a chance to prove themselves and this is what you get. Now, I would have to convene a court-martial and he would have to stand with his nose in the...

BAM BAM BAM!

"Slim, get out of bed!"

17

Holy smokes, we had problems bigger than Drover. Had you forgotten the intruder? If you don't start paying attention, we're going to drop you from the next assignment. One Drover on this team is all we can stand.

CHAPTER THREE

Not a Robot

Slim was coming down the hall, tucking in his shirttail. Good. He could take the lead on this deal and I would provide backup. I dived under the...that is, I found myself beneath the coffee table and started pumping out some cover fire. Awesome barks.

He went to the door and yanked it open. There stood...hmmm, it wasn't a robot, as you might have thought. It was an old guy: white hair, bushy eyebrows, smoky gray eyes, and red suspenders holding up khaki pants that bagged in the seat. I sent this info to Data Control and got an ID: Woodrow, Viola's daddy.

See? What did I tell you? We've never had a robot show up at Slim's place and probably never will. I've tried to drill this into the troops: stick with the facts and don't let your imagination run wild. Drover is the very worst about making a mountain out of a mohair.

Anyway, there stood Viola's daddy. Slim said, "Why…Woodrow. What a nice surprise."

"Did I get you out of bed?"

"Heck no, been up for hours. I was updating my tally book."

"We need to talk."

"Well sure, come on in. You want some coffee?"

"No, I've coffeed. Been up since five."

Slim brought a chair from the kitchen. When Woodrow sat down, it collapsed, I mean sank into a heap of rubble. Slim had to pull him out. "Sorry, Woodrow. I've been meaning to fix that thing." He brought another chair from the kitchen.

Woodrow tested it. "Is this one safe?"

"Here, you take the easy chair and I'll…" Woodrow waved him off and sat in the kitchen chair. It held.

Slim flopped down in his big easy chair. "Well, what can I do for you?"

"Are you going to marry my daughter or not?"

Wow, that killed every fly in the room. Slim's adam's apple jumped and he blinked his eyes. "What?"

"Are you going to marry my daughter or not?"

"Well, Woodrow, yes, but I need to save up some money."

"She's been wearing that ring for six months and I ain't seen any signs of progress."

"Saving money is kind of slow on cowboy wages."

"I told you that from the beginning. You can't afford a parakeet, much less a wife. If y'all wait till you can afford to get hitched, she'll be eighty years old. Maybe you ought to start robbing banks."

"Well, I hadn't thought of that."

"Or get some heifers, calve 'em out, and start building your own cow herd. I'll give you the pasture for free."

"Woodrow, if I wrote a check for heifers, they'd send me to the pen. My checking account's in pretty sad shape."

Woodrow's eyes were crackling and he leaned forward. "I'll give you the danged heifers!"

Now a little fire came into Slim's eyes. "That's nice, but I don't want free heifers from you or anyone else. I can take care of my own business."

"Then do it! Go talk to a banker."

"I don't have one. I like bankers even less than doctors."

"Well, I've got one and I've used him plenty. He loans money to people who want to make something of themselves."

Slim took a deep breath. "Woodrow, if your banker looked at my financial statement, he wouldn't quit laughing for a week."

"I'll co-sign the note."

Slim's eyes bugged out. "You ain't going to co-sign my note! I ain't going to borrow money to buy cows I can't afford!"

There was a moment of deadly silence, then the old man's lips twitched into a wicked little smile. "That's just what I thought you'd say." He pushed himself out of the chair and headed for the door.

"Sorry, Woodrow. I appreciate the offer."

"That's all right. Viola didn't figure you'd go for it, so she'll talk to the banker herself. See you around."

He went out the door. Slim sat there for a moment, then flew out of his chair. It kind of caught me by surprise and, well, I fired off three barks. He sailed out the door, I followed, and we caught up with Woodrow as he was about to get into his pickup.

"Hey, did you say she's going to sign a note to buy some heifers?"

"That's right, ten head of bred heifers. She'll meet with the banker. You don't have to do a thing but stay out here and preach thrift to that dog." He glared down at me through shaggy brows. "You'd better preach good, 'cause he don't look too smart."

What? Who?

He climbed into the cab and started the motor. Slim banged on the window. Woodrow rolled it down. "What?"

Slim dug his hands into his pockets and took a big breath. "Okay, I'll talk to the frazzling banker."

"You sure?"

"I'm sure I got ambushed. When does this take place?"

"We'll pick you up in an hour. Take a bath and do something with that hair. Do you own any decent clothes? Wear 'em. Just because you're a pauper don't mean you have to look like one."

He drove off, didn't roll up his window or say goodbye, and left us in a cloud of dust. Slim fanned the air in front of his face and muttered, "Thanks, Woodrow, for putting me on the road to the Poor House."

He trudged back to the porch, walking like a sad old man, all bent over and frowning. I must admit that I didn't understand any of that conversation, except the part about taking a bath. Maybe that was it. He had to take a bath and it wasn't even Saturday. That can put a guy into a dark mood, I guess.

It really didn't matter if I understood or not. Dogs don't understand half of what goes on with our people, but that's just part of the job. What matters is that we're there to walk beside them. We're *there* when they need us.

I would walk with Slim all the way to the bathtub and give him comfort in his time of need. I might even drag his jeans into another room and fling them around in my jaws. I kind of enjoy doing that.

When he reached the front door, he speared me with his eyes and said, "No."

No what? I hadn't done anything.

"You stay outside. Stubtail will be right out."

Well, gee, that seemed kind of harsh. How could he take a bath without...he went inside. A few minutes later, the door opened and Stubtail came flying out and landed on the porch.

He seemed on the virgil of tears. "He yelled at me and threw me out of the house!"

I marched over to him. "Good. Now we can get started on your court martial. Sit down and show some respect. This court finds you guilty of all charges."

He blinked. "What charges?"

"The charges of which you've been charged of which, mainly being a little chicken."

His head sank. "Oh, that. I was hoping you didn't notice."

"Of course I noticed! Every member of this jury saw you run from the field of battle."

"Oh rats."

"Do you admit the charge of the charges?"

"Might as well, if everybody saw it." He started sniffling. "But you didn't see the worst part."

"You mean...there was more?"

"Yeah, but I don't want to talk about it. I'm so ashamed!"

I began pacing in front of the witness, I mean, this sounded bad. "Okay, let's get this over with. Tell this court exactly what happened, and don't forget that you're under oath."

"You mean like oathmeal?"

"Exactly. Oathmeal is the most honest of all cereals, and that's what we expect from your testimony. No whoppers, in other words."

"Oh drat."

"Please don't use naughty language. Go on."

He hung his head and wiped a tear out of his eye. "I wet under Slim's bed."

Those words hit me like a wooden nickel falling from the sky. I stopped pacing and stared at him. "You wet...Drover, how could you do such a thing?"

"It was easy. You told me there was a robot on the porch and it scared me so bad, I couldn't hold it."

"Why would you want to hold a robot?"

"No, the water."

"Oh. Well, you wasted your water. There wasn't a robot on the porch."

"That makes it even worse."

I paced around him and pondered all the evidence. I found it hard to keep from laughing. "This is ha ha shameful. Your honor, we the jury have come to a verdict."

"Are you talking to me?"

"No, just listen and keep your trap shut. Your honor, we find the defendant guilty of being a little chicken and wetting under Slim's bed."

"Oh no!"

"But it's so funny, we recommend no punishment."

His jaw dropped. "No fooling? I don't have to stand with my nose in the corner?"

"Drover, this is hilarious. Did Slim find the puddle?"

"Not yet."

"Then you're home free. Congratulations, son, you've beat the system by being a complete goose. This court is adjourned!"

CHAPTER FOUR

Slim Wears a Suit

So there you are, a little glimpse into the inner workings of the Security Division. Most of our cases involve serious crimes and serious crinimals, but this one...

How can you stay mad at a little mutt who's so scared of robots, he wets under the bed?

I know, I know, he went chicken in combat and hid under the bed, but sometimes Justice must be merciful to noodle-brains. There's a time to stick their noses in the corner, sure, but once in a while, Justice must pause and laugh its head off.

Anyway, we disposed of an important case and it was time to get back to work. Actually, there wasn't any work, because Slim was getting ready to go somewhere and do something, so we sat on the porch and werp wonky donut snork.

I must have slipped into a light doze, but don't forget that I'd been in court most of the morning. That wears you down. I was awakened by a name calling my voice.

"Hank?"

"We're away from the phone. At the sound of the tone, leave me alone."

"What a cute rhyme!"

"Figgy pudding."

"I need to ask you something."

I cranked open one eye and saw a dog. "Who are you and who gave you my number?"

"I'm Drover, remember me?"

I blinked all four eyes and glanced around. "Wait. You're the one who wet under the bed?"

"Yeah, but I don't want to talk about it."

"Good. Where are we?"

"Slim's porch."

I pushed myself to a sitting position, glanced around, and took a big yawn and stretch. "I must have drifted off for a minute."

"You were zonked out for an hour. You were twitching and making squeaky sounds. I heard 'em myself."

I gave him a smoldering glare. "I don't make squeaky sounds. You need to get your ears fixed.

Why did you wake me up?"

"Well..." He rolled his eyes around. "I'm not feeling so good."

"You're sick? Open your mouth and say ah-h-h-h." He opened his beak and I peered inside.

"Has your tongue always been pink?"

He nodded. "I hink hoe."

"Close your mouth. When did you start feeling bad?"

"It was right after you said something about germs. I think I caught some of 'em."

"I didn't say anything about germs. Why would I be talking about germs?"

"I don't know, but you said, 'This court is a germ,' and that's when it all started."

I stared into the great emptiness of his eyes. "Drover, is this a pathetic attempt at humor?"

"Heck no. There's nothing funny about germs."

"When you were a kid, did your mother think you were strange?"

"Well, let me think. She thought I was a lazy bum."

"She was right, but you're also a hypocardiac. You get sick when you're not sick."

"Yeah, but..."

I stuck my nose in his face. "I didn't say anything about germs. I said, and please pay attention, I said, 'This court is now adjourned.' Adjourned! It meant that your court martial was over."

He tilted his head to the side and squeezed up a silly grin. "No fooling? So...I'm okay, I'm not sick?"

"You're not sick in the usual sense. You're weird, and we need to have a long talk about that."

I had planned to give him The Heavy Lecture about his weirdness, but that got interrupted when a strange pickup came creeping toward the house. My head shot up and I activated sensors. I had never seen this vehicle before, so you can guess what happened next. My lecture went out the window.

"Uh oh, Bogies at two o'clock! It's time to launch all dogs, let's go!"

I pushed the throttle up to Turbo Five, dived off the porch, and went streaking out to intercept the Bogies, and you should have heard those jet engines! Awesome roar. I made contact, gave 'em a burst of Warning Barks, and kept 'em under cerveza until they parked in front of Slim's shack.

The driver honked the horn. I couldn't tell if it was a hostile honk or a friendly honk, so I stood my ground and kept 'em covered. The window on the driver's side window rolled down and I saw... holy smokes, it was Miss Viola! She looked fabulous and gave me a big smile and said, "Hi, Hank!"

See? What have I been telling you? She was

crazy about me and she'd come to pay me a visit! I rushed forward, hopped my front paws on the side of the pickup, and leaned upward to receive Rubs and Pats. I got 'em, but also heard a deep growl inside the cab. "Don't let him scratch my paint job!"

Okay, that was her grouchy old daddy, and Viola said, "Hank, get down." No problem. Anything for her.

Slim came out the front door, and get this. He was wearing a suit and tie and a clean hat! Incredible. I mean, he looked halfway civilized. I hardly recognized him. But he wasn't wearing a happy face. His lips looked like nails and he walked with his head down.

When he opened the passenger-side door, Viola said, "My, don't you look handsome!"

"I feel like I'm going to a funeral. Mine."

He got in and they drove off and didn't come back until late afternoon, which left me alone on the porch with the guy whose mother thought he was a lazy bum. Boy, what a long day!

But I survived and was there to meet the pickup when they came back, and gave 'em an escort to the house. Slim and Viola got out and walked to the porch. They were holding hands. I'll admit that it made me a little jealous, her giving him so much attention, but I tried to be mature about it. I mean, they were engaged.

She said, "See, that wasn't so bad. I was proud of you, sitting across the desk from the banker. That was very brave."

"The way Brady looked at me, I felt like a chicken thief."

"Oh, that's the silliest thing I ever heard! Slim, every young couple goes through this, starting out. We'll work together and it'll be fine. Two calf crops and we can burn the note." They climbed the steps and stopped at the door. She looked him over. "You should dress up more often."

"When we burn the note, the suit goes into the fire."

The horn honked and we heard Woodrow's growly voice. "Hurry up, girl, I've got to gather the eggs!"

She stood on tip-toes and kissed him on the cheek. "You did great. See you soon."

Eight seconds after she drove away, Slim ripped off his necktie and unbuttoned his collar. He leaned against a pillar post and looked off into the distance. "Hank, I'm inching closer to the altar. Should I be glad or scared silly?"

You know, I was proud that he had asked my

opinion, but since I had no idea what he was talking about, all I could do was answer with Slow Caring Wags on the tail section. He didn't even notice my wags. Oh well. Sometimes SCW works and sometimes it flops.

He changed back into his work clothes, went to his mailbox on the county road, and retrieved a week's collection of mail: a picture show calendar, grocery store ads, a newsletter from the church, and the latest issue of *Livestock Weekly*. Back at the house, he spent an hour studying the "Cattle For Sale" section in LW and making phone calls to ranchers who had heifers to sell.

The next morning, he hooked up the flatbed pickup to the 24' gooseneck trailer, and off we went to Lipscomb County to buy ten head of heifers. He insisted that I go along and ride shotgun on this deal, and I was glad to do it. To be real honest, I needed a break from Drover.

But there was another reason I volunteered for the mission. Can you guess? Heh heh. Miss Viola went along too and, well, you know how it was between us. She was engaged to Slim, but also crazy about me. In fact, I take credit for bringing them together.

Think about it. Slim owned no land, couldn't dance, was always bachelor-broke, ate bad food, and had all the charm of a rock, but he had partnered with a dog who was...well, everything you'd want: handsome, strong, smart, brave, loyal, smart, brave, and handsome.

So, yes, I take a lot of credit for bringing them together. I'm not saying that I wanted to steal her away, but I never passed up an opportunity to ride in the pickup with her. Sometimes, when things were just right, I was able to slither into her lap, and those were delicious moments.

I was with them when they picked up the heifers, and watched Slim write Lance Bussard a check for eight thousand bucks. His hand trembled and his face was pale, and he told Lance, "Just keep running it through till it clears the bank."

Maybe that was a joke. Anyway, everyone laughed.

CHAPTER FIVE

A Bad Wind

We loaded the heifers and hauled them to Viola's place and turned them out in a pasture that Woodrow was furnishing at no charge. In other words, they were getting free pasture, which lowered their expense. After frost, Slim bought sacks of cubed feed, and through the winter, he and Viola fed them twenty pounds of cake every day.

In February, the heifers started calving, and you know how it is with first-calf heifers. They're young and small, and sometimes they have trouble delivering that first calf. When they get close to calving, you have to watch them day and night, and help them if they have problems.

Viola went down to the calving barn every

four hours and checked the heavy heifers, and on two occasions, she had to call Slim to come help her pull a calf. By the first of March, they had calved out all ten heifers, and ten healthy calves were romping around on the feed ground. Slim and Viola were proud. That was the start on their cow herd and the future.

That brings us to the sixth of March, a day that nobody around here will ever forget. It was early morning at Slim's place and the wind was blowing outside. That's all the wind ever does in March. It blows from the north, then it blows from the south, the southwest, and the west, back and forth like a fiddle bow, and we're the fiddle.

We were sick of it. It had been going on for a week, every day, wind and dust. Couldn't the wind find something better to do? Those of us in the Security Division had been pulling double shifts, I mean, hour after hour of standing out in the cold and blasting away with Anti-Wind Barking, but nothing had worked.

But today, wind was worse than usual. It had blown hard through the night and was making some creepy sounds in the house: whistles, pops, groans, and rumbles. A dog notices things like that, and Slim noticed. He cocked his head and listened.

I was watching him and gave a bark to let him

know that I'd heard them too.

"Will you dry up?"

Oh brother. You know, trying to communicate with that guy in the morning is a waste of effort. What's the point in having a dog...never mind.

Dressed in his Morning Attire (boxer shorts, T-shirt, and bare feet), he went to the door and stepped out on the porch. I didn't offer to go with him. Once a dog has been rebeeked, he loses his enthusiasm for the job and stops caring. Rebuked, I guess it should be.

Our Normal Procedure calls for the dog to follow his people wherever they go, whether that's room to room or out on the porch, and to show some interest in their lives. *We follow them because we care.*

But he had ruined that by screeching at me and telling me to dry up, and I no longer cared. Dogs have feelings too. We're not just furniture.

He came back into the house. "That's a bad wind."

Did I care? No. I turned my back on him.

He noticed. "Hey, pooch, it's liable to be a bad day for fires."

Oh, he wanted his dog back now, someone to sit there and listen to him ramble about wind and fire. Too bad.

"You get your feelings hurt too easy."

I had nothing to say to him, nothing.

"You want to split a cookie?"

Huh?

"Viola made me a batch of oatmeal-raisin cookies. I might share one."

Let's be clear about this. Nobody buys me off with half a cookie, but one of the most endearing qualities of cowdogs is that we *forgive*. All dogs get their feelings hurt once in a while, and ordinary mutts hold a grudge. They pout like little cry-babies. Cowdogs see the big picture and rise above such childish behavior.

Somebody had to show some maturity. Maybe Slim and I could work out our differences. Okay, sure.

He went to the spot where he had stashed the cookies, and I made careful note of the location: on the dinner table. Heh heh. A guy never knows when the opportunity might arise...no, let's don't go there. I wouldn't want the little children to get the idea that...just skip it.

Viola had packed the cookies in a pretty little box lined with red tissue paper, and there it slurp on the table, there it sat. Slim gave me a hard look. "Don't get any big ideas, pooch."

What! I couldn't believe he'd said that. Did he think I was some kind of half-crazed cookie gobbler? Oh brother.

He opened the box and brought out a cookie, broke it in half and studied the two halves. He stuffed the bigger half into his mouth and pitched the other one in the air. I tracked it on radar for half a second, launched myself and snapped it right out of the skyosphere. SNARF!

Slim chuckled. "Heh. You looked like Larry Bird on that one."

I looked like a bird? Well, so did he, standing there with his stork legs.

Anyway, it was a great catch and a great cookie, and you'll never hear me complain about getting the smaller half.

Slim went off to his bedroom to put on some clothes and I drifted into the living room to stir Squeakbox out of bed. As you might expect, I showed a high level of sensitivity, I mean, he's very fragile in the morning.

I gave him Train Horns in the left ear.

BWONK!

"Arise and sing, Half Stepper! We've got a ranch to run."

Hee hee. What a show! He went off like a box of mousetraps and flew eighteen inches off the floor. When his eyeballs quit rolling around, he croaked, "I smell cookies!"

"Hey, great job on the smeller, but you don't get one."

"No fair! I never get cookies."

"Because you spend most of your waking hours asleep. Let's go to work."

We followed Slim out of the house, and right away got slapped by a west wind that was loaded with dust, sand, bits of grass, and hay leaves. Tumbleweeds loped across the gravel drive in front of the house and Slim's hat went airborne. If it hadn't snagged on a fence, it might have rolled all the way to Arkansas.

Drover let out a pitiful moan and went into a sneezing fit, I mean five in a row, almost blew off the end of his nose. "I hate this wind! And dow by siduses are really aggdig ub! I wad do go bag to bed! Helb!"

Before I could give him a lecture on the Importance of Good Work Habits, he parked himself in the southwest corner of the porch, curled up in a little white ball, and covered his ears with his paws.

Well, we wouldn't be getting any work out of Drover today—not that we ever did—and that's where he would spend the rest of the day.

Slim chased down his hat and managed to open the pickup door and hold on to it, so the wind didn't tear it off the hinges. "Load up, pooch, let's go feed cattle!"

Aye aye, sir! I went flying into the cab. Slim dived in, tugged on the door, and finally got it shut. The wind was blowing so hard, we could feel it rocking the pickup. Slim muttered, "Man alive, I hope nobody makes a spark today. Dry as we are, the whole Panhandle could burn up."

As we drove away from the house, I looked back and saw a ball of white fur quivering on the porch. I thought, "What a funny little guy!" It never crossed my mind that he might be there when...or that I might never...you just don't think it will ever turn out that way.

That's all we can say about it right now.

We were feeding cattle every day because the weather was still chilly and we hadn't gotten any winter moisture, so the grass hadn't greened up yet. I mean, we were as dry as a powder house. Until we got some rain or snow, our grass would stay brown and the cattle would need some protein in their diet, especially cows that were nursing calves.

We drove to the county road and turned right at the mail box, then chugged along at fifteen miles an hour to ranch headquarters. It was only a three-mile drive but it seemed longer. Slim had never been one to rush into a new day, and he sure wasn't pushing things now. He still had coffee to drink.

Up ahead, a big brown tumbleweed came rolling down the middle of the road. Slim steered the pickup to the left, so as to miss it, but the wind shifted and we met it head-on. It went under the pickup and got hung, and we drove into headquarters with that thing making an awful scraping sound.

I was pretty sure Slim would stop and clean it out. I waited and watched. He slurped coffee and drove on.

Was this some kind of clue or dark omen of things to come? Maybe not. Sometimes a tumbleweed is just a tumbleweed.

CHAPTER SIX

Smoke!

Loper was down at the corrals when we drove up, and he met us when we got out of the pickup. He wore a scowl. "You're fixing to lose a wheel bearing on that pickup."

"I don't think so."

"I heard you coming fifty yards away. I've got ears and I know when a bearing's going out."

"It ain't a bearing."

"You know what happens when you burn up a bearing?"

"Wheel falls off."

"That's right, and if you happen to be driving down the road, it can be hard on ranch equipment. You'd better run it in the barn, pull all four wheels, and check for a hot bearing."

"I'll bet you five bucks it ain't a wheel bearing."
Loper glared at him. "Since when did you know squat about grease and bearings?"

"Five bucks, American cash money, says it ain't a wheel bearing."

"I'll take it. Let's go pull the tires. You drive. If a wheel falls off, I want you to get the credit."

"Loper, look under the front end."

"What?"

"Just look."

Loper bent down and looked. When he straightened up, his sour expression had deepened. "You could have said you hit a tumbleweed."

"I didn't hit the tumbleweed, it hit me, and you were on such a snort about wheel bearings, I didn't want to interrupt the sermon."

Loper shook his head and looked away. "I'm sure there's a simple reason why you didn't pull it out."

"It ain't bothering me."

"So...how long are you going to drive around with that thing scraping under the pickup?"

"Till it comes a-loose, I guess."

"Pull it out before it drives me nuts."

"Okay, but you owe me five bucks."

"I'll include it in your severance package. Hurry up, we've got work to do."

Those guys go on like this all the time. If you didn't know better, you might think they were ready to duke it out, but it never seems to amount to much. If they asked my opinion…but they never do, so we can skip on to something else.

But I will go on record as saying that they waste a lot of time, yapping back and forth at each other. There.

Once Slim had removed the tumbleweed, he and I drove to the feed barn and loaded twenty sacks of feed into the bed of his pickup, then began the routine of feeding all the pastures on the east side of the ranch. The wind was really howling and Slim had to put a shovel on top of the empty paper sacks to keep them from blowing all over the ranch.

Boy, it was a nasty day. The cattle looked wind-blown and miserable. Slim's eyes were red-rimmed from the dust, and he couldn't keep his hat from blowing off. You know, cowboys look pretty silly, chasing after their hats. There's something undignified about a grown man with big feet and skinny legs, chasing after a hat like he was trying to catch a rabbit.

After the tenth time, he finally smartened up, parked his hat in the pickup, and pulled on a baseball cap that would stay on his head. As windy as it is in the Panhandle, I don't know why those guys waste money on an expensive hat anyway.

It seems kind of extravagant, doesn't it? They could be using that money to improve the ranch. They could buy steaks for their dogs or at least put their money into a higher grade of dog food, something better than Cheapo and Co-op.

On the other hand, he looked pretty silly in that cap. I mean, there's a certain dignity about a man who wears a nice cowboy hat. It tells the world that he's got pride and good taste in clothes. A few sweat stains along the crown reveal that he might have even done some work.

A baseball cap tells the world, "This guy's too cheap to buy a decent hat and too dumb to know that he looks dumb in a cap that advertises chain saws."

There, I've said my piece on fashion.

It must have been around two o'clock. Slim had just poured out two sacks of feed and we were walking back to the pickup. He stopped and lifted his head. "I smell smoke."

I turned my nose into the wind and switched on Snifforadar. I was picking it up too. Smoke from a grass fire.

"Get in, dog, we'd better find out where that's

coming from."

We were down along the creek, don't you see, and didn't have a good view of the country to the south and west. We drove north and followed a feed trail that led to the top of a caprock, parked there and stepped out. Slim shaded his eyes and looked off to the west. So did I and we both saw it: a thin layer of white smoke in the distance, above the horizon.

Slim swallowed hard. "That's a grass fire and if the wind doesn't shift, we're going to be in the path of it. This is liable to be a bad day, Hank, maybe a real bad day. Load up!"

Remember what I said about Slim poking along and driving slow? Well, he got over that. We went ripping down those pasture roads as fast as he could drive, I mean fish-tailing around curves and all four tires off the ground on bumps. It scared the liver right out of me, and I'm not scared of anything.

If Drover had been there, I guarantee he would have had made a puddle on the floorboard. We were lucky he didn't come.

By the time we reached headquarters, that band of smoke had moved over the sun and turned it an ugly shade of yellow-brown, and the burned smell had gotten stronger. We saw Loper coming

out of the house with an armload of stuff and loading it into the car.

When we reached him, Slim said, "What's the news? How bad is it?"

"Bad. Sheriff's office called and said to evacuate. It started east of Borger and it's coming this way. The leading edge is fifteen miles wide and it's getting bigger by the minute, totally out of control."

"Good honk. What should we do?"

Loper wiped the sweat off his face. "I'm sending Sally May and the kids to town. They'll have to go the back way in case the highway is closed. I'll take my pickup and open pasture gates on the way out, so the cattle can drift."

"I'll start filling the spray rig with water."

Loper looked him straight in the eye and shook his head. "Forget the spray rig. This is like no fire we've seen before. It's a killer. Deputy Kile said, 'Drop everything and run like a rabbit.'"

"And with that advice, you're going to open pasture gates. Most rabbits don't do that."

"I'm the guy who signed the note at the bank, but don't worry, I'm getting out of here too." He looked off to the west. "Look at that smoke cloud!"

"Has anyone talked to Viola or her folks?"

Loper shook his head. "Sally May tried to call, no answer."

"I'll check on 'em. Woodrow won't leave, I know he won't. He makes a mule look like an honor student."

"Well, *make* him leave! Tie him up and throw him into the back of the pickup. If that fire gets into the creek bottom, there won't be a house left standing. Get out of here! I'll see you in town."

"Don't try to be a hero. You wouldn't make good barbecue."

Loper laughed.

Sally May and the children came out of the house. Alfred was lugging a suitcase and Sally May carried the baby and an overnight bag. She paused at the gate and looked back at the house, then hurried to the car.

She put Molly into the car seat and went back to the gate. "Pete? Here, kitty kitty! Pete?" She glanced around the yard. No cat. "Pete! Come here, now!"

What have I been telling you about cats? Call 'em and they disappear. Tell 'em to buzz off and they'll wrap around your ankles. I didn't wish the cat any bad luck, but it appeared that he might get some anyway.

Slim trotted to his pickup. He didn't call me but he didn't need to. There was no way I was going to get left behind. We dived inside the cab and roared away from the house, made a ripping right turn at the mail box, and headed east on the county road.

I won't be bashful: I was scared. If you're not scared, something's wrong.

Evacuation

If I ever complain about Slim driving too slow, please wash my mouth out with soap. Remember that low-water crossing east of headquarters, where the creek runs over a cement slab? When you hit that sucker at forty miles an hour, it does bad things to a pickup.

We bottomed out on the shocks and springs, heard awful noises, and things went flying around inside the cab: fencing pliers, gloves we hadn't seen in years, a bottle of vaccine, two pounds of dust, twenty-seven miller moths, and me.

I scraped myself off the floorboard and beamed him a glare. "Will you slow this thing down? The fire won't have a chance to kill us, because you're going to..."

I choked on the dust and couldn't finish my sentence. Whilst I coughed, Slim gave me a solemn look and said, "Hang on, pooch."

Oh right, sure, hang on. I returned to my shotgun-side seat and...good grief, we were fixing to smash head-on into an army surplus six-by-six fire truck! Have you ever seen one of those things up close? They're huge! Well, this was IT. Our geese were cooked.

Slim hit the brakes and swerved into the ditch on the right side. I got spilled into the dashboard, but we missed the six-by-six. Whew!

It was a truck from the Lipscomb Volunteer Fire Department, and right behind it came two red fire trucks with lights flashing. These were from Canadian, and behind them came a water truck from Higgins. They were all heading for the front lines, carrying men dressed in green fire suits.

At last, and through some miracle, we reached Viola's place and were still alive. I was never so glad to hop out of a pickup, and swore I would never say another critical word about Slim's slow driving.

We didn't see any signs of people, so Slim trotted to the house and I followed. I can't be blamed that he tripped on me and fell into the flower bed. "Bird brain, get out of the way!"

Hey, in a fire emergency, every man and dog on this outfit has to wake up and pay attention to his business. I couldn't be blamed, but of course he blamed me anyway. That's what dogs are for, it seems. Any time there's a mess, call in the dogs and smear 'em with blame.

Viola came out the front door and saw him sprawled across her mother's flower bed. "Slim? What are you doing?"

He picked himself up and brushed off his jeans. "Well, I was on my way to find you, but Jughead tripped me. Sorry about your mother's flowers."

"The sheriff's department is evacuating everyone on the creek."

"That's why I'm here. Y'all need to get out, now."

"I know. Mom is packing a few things, but Daddy..."

"Where is he?"

She pointed to the south side of the house, where Woodrow was dragging a garden hose. "He says he's going to stay and fight the fire. Maybe you could talk to him."

"I'd sooner talk to a flat rock."

"Slim! Try. Please."

"Okay, I'll try, but y'all need to get on the road."

"And you?"

"Once I get Woodrow loaded, I'll follow you out. Did you see our heifers this morning?"

"Yes. They were down on the south end of the Cottonwood pasture. Slim, you're not..."

"No, I just wondered. Go on, scat."

Viola went back into the house. Slim took a

deep breath, licked his lips, hitched up his jeans, and marched like a brave soldier to Woodrow, who was spraying the side of the house with the hose. He must have lost his hat in the wind, and his white hair was flying around on his head.

He gave Slim a hard glance. "Grab a hose and make yourself useful."

"Woodrow, you need to leave."

"I've been fighting grass fires all my life and never been burned up yet. Grab a hose."

"Woodrow, this ain't just a grass fire, it's a *wildfire*. It's fifteen miles wide and has a fifty mile an hour wind behind it. The garden hose won't do one bit of good. You need to leave with your wife and daughter."

Woodrow stiffened. "My granddaddy built this house. I was born in that upstairs bedroom, and I ain't leaving. If it goes, I go with it."

"Woodrow, the sheriff's department has ordered an evacuation. Is there any part of that you don't understand? Law enforcement says to get out!"

Woodrow gave a chuckle. "Well, law enforcement ain't here, are they?" He went right on spraying the house. Slim shook his head and muttered under his breath. It looked hopeless, but then...

A car pulled up in front of the house. It had

flashing lights on the roof and appeared to be, well, law enforcement. A man in a uniform stepped out and came toward us.

Hey, that was Chief Deputy Kile, and he looked mighty serious. He and Slim exchanged nods and the deputy pointed to the big cloud of smoke to the west. "You can't believe how fast that fire's moving. Never saw anything like it. We need to get these folks out of here, and I'm talking about *fast*."

"Bobby, I tried to explain it to Woodrow. He said he ain't leaving. My next idea was to knock him in the head with a ballpeen hammer and load him with the tractor."

The deputy smiled. "I'll talk to him." He tapped Woodrow on the shoulder. The old man was surprised to see him. "Afternoon, Woodrow. The governor of Texas has declared this a disaster area."

"Is that right?"

"He told me to come out here and make sure you complied with the evacuation order."

"Yeah, and bird dogs fly."

"We've been told by certain parties that you're a stubborn old man and hard to deal with, so I brought handcuffs, just in case."

"Well, you can tell the governor..."

The deputy brought out a set of handcuffs

from his belt. "I'd rather not use them, but one way or another, you need to get on the road."

Woodrow scorched him with a glare. "Who do you think you are? You're just a snot-nose kid with a tin star on his shirt!" Deputy Kile said nothing. "I was raised here and I've never run from a fire." Deputy Kile said nothing. The old man licked his lips. "Is it that bad?"

"Yes sir, worse than you can imagine."

"You're getting too big for your britches." Woodrow dropped the hose. "I'll leave the water running. Maybe it'll help." With his head bent low, he walked to the front door, just as Viola and her mother came out with clothes and a few boxes.

Slim and Deputy Kile gave sighs of relief, and Slim patted him on the shoulder. "By grabs, you got his attention. I take back all the bad things I've said about you."

Just then, we heard the roar of diesel engines and saw three big motor graders heading west on the country road. The deputy nodded. "Good, they made it. They'll plow fire guards and the Forest Service is sending tankers from Abilene. Maybe we can save a few houses."

Slim and I walked him to his car. We could hear a lot of noise on the police radio. The deputy said, "Get 'em on the road. You too. This is the real deal."

"Thanks, Bobby, and take care of yourself."

The deputy got into his car and drove west, toward the huge cloud of smoke. Viola came over to us. "We're ready…I guess. What do you take? Should I ride with you?"

"No, you go with your folks and drive. In case we get separated, go east to the highway, then north and make your way to town. I'll catch up with you there."

She looked at the cloud in the west. "I hope they can save the house. See you in town."

She jumped into the car. Woodrow rode in the front and Rosella sat in the back with the two dogs, Black and Jack, and off they went, east down the county road.

I started toward the pickup. I mean, the smoke was getting thick and I was ready to get out of there.

Huh?

Slim was walking toward the barn. Hey, what was the deal? I barked. He kept walking, almost as though…

Surely he wasn't going to try to move the heifers.

This was crazy! The smoke was so thick now, you couldn't see more than a couple hundred feet...AND HE WAS WALKING TOWARD THE BARN?

Well, if he'd lost his brain, too bad. I hadn't lost mine and I had no intention of...I glanced around. Everyone but us had left and I couldn't drive the pickup.

Gulp.

Anyway, as I was saying, any cowdog worth his salt will stick with his people through thick and thicker, I mean, it's just bred into us, so, yes, I kicked up the jets and caught up with him as he opened the corral gate.

He looked down at me. "I should have sent you with Viola. Sorry, pup, I have one last job to do, and we need to be quick about it."

A sorrel mare stood in the pen, chewing on some alfalfa hay. She was sway-backed and had ribs showing and looked almost as old as Woodrow. Slim said, "I'll bet she ain't been rode in ten years, but maybe she won't buck me off."

He went inside the shed and rattled around, looking for tack. He found an old dusty saddle with leather as stiff as shingles, and a bridle hanging on a nail. The reins were hard and dry and had cobwebs on them. He grabbed 'em and had the mare saddled in five minutes, then ducked back into the shed, found one spur, and buckled it on his boot.

He led the mare out the gate, tightened the cinch one more notch, and swung up into the saddle. "So far, so good. Let's ride!"

Gulp.

CHAPTER EIGHT

Racing the Fire

Okay, Slim was horseback on an old skinny mare and poked her with a spur. She pinned back her ears, wrung her tail, and crow-hopped. He slapped her with the bridle reins and I guess she figured out that she wasn't hauling Woodrow or one of the grandkids. She straightened up and trotted south.

Those ten heifers he and Viola had bought and calved out were staying in a pasture south of the corral. It was good bottomland on the east side of a little creek, and it had grown a bunch of tall grass last summer, thick and knee-high on a man.

It made great pasture for a bunch of first-calf heifers. It also had tons of dry standing fuel for a prairie fire, and that's the kind of thing nobody ever thought about until today. Always before, a rancher took pride in a pasture of tall grass. Today, that tall dry grass didn't look so great.

Through the smoke, we saw the heifers about half a mile away. Slim tried to squeeze some speed out of the old mare but didn't have much luck. A slow trot was the best he could get. All at once, I lost sight of the heifers and the air got thick with smoke. Slim noticed too, and looked over his shoulder.

I'll never forget that sight. Off to the west, the smoke had become a wall, and it was flashing with red and yellow light. I mean, we couldn't see flames, but they were there inside the smoke— big and coming fast!

"Good honk, it's already here! Hank, I don't know if we can outrun that thing or not."

Yeah, well, why didn't we stop talking about it and find out? Because it had come down to that.

You might say that the fire built a fire under that old mare. When she saw what was coming, she must have decided that she was younger than she thought. Slim used his one spur and the old mare took care of the rest, I mean, she was hauling the mail out of there.

I had to hit Turbo Five to stay up with her and, fellers, we were covering some country. I figured we were doing okay, I mean we'd finally gotten the old nag out of a trot, but Slim glanced back over his shoulder and yelled, "We can't outrun that thing!"

That sent a shock out to the end of my tail. Good grief! IF WE COULDN'T OUTRUN IT, WHAT DID THAT LEAVE?

The smoke was so thick now, I could hardly breath. I could feel the heat and hear the crackling roar behind me. Slim was right, we were running full-speed and the fire was catching up with us, and in that sea of tall grass, there was no place to hide.

We always assume that we'll get twelve chapters out of a story, but maybe it doesn't work that way all the time. What shall we do here? If we quit the story in the middle of Chapter Eight, we'll never know how it turned out, but if we keep going, well, something bad might happen, really bad.

Do we dare take the chance? Should we quit or go on?

I knew you'd say that.

Okay, we'll give it a shot, but it's going to be scary, so you need to get prepared. Go to the bathroom, drink some milk, and find a big solid chair you can hang onto.

Ready?

Okay, it looked bad. No, it looked worse than bad. Hopeless. If I'd been out there by myself, let's be honest here, I think the fire would have gotten me. I mean, I had worked up several Anti-Fire Barking Procedures, and they'd worked pretty well on fires in the past, but this inferno was in a class by itself.

And I was facing the wrong direction. See, you can't bark-out a fire when you're running from it, just doesn't work. Imagine trying to douse a fire with a water hose pointed the wrong direction. Same deal. My Bark Launcher was point east and the fire was coming from the west, so the Security Division was out of the fight.

Lucky for me, I was out there with a guy...you know, Slim doesn't always come across as the brightest candle on the Christmas tree. He wasn't at the top of his class in school, and I've heard him say that he enjoyed the eighth grade so much, he stayed there for three years. That might have been a joke, but the truth is, sometimes he does things that seem...let's be kind and say *odd*.

But on that one day, in that moment of greatest peril, he made a genius decision. We were running flat-out and losing ground. Up ahead, he spotted a little ravine that was about ten feet deep, and steered the mare toward it. She stopped on the edge and wouldn't go down, so he bailed out of the saddle, took the reins, and led her down.

She followed, and so did I, and nobody had to pull my reins. I took a flying leap and crash-landed into a clump of skunk brush. No problem there. I had never been so glad to hug a skunk brush.

Down in the ravine, the smoke wasn't bad and we had some air to breathe, but we could hear the roar and crackle of the fire, and it was LOUD. Scary. Slim pulled his shirt up over his head and lay flat on the ground. I did the same, only I didn't have a shirt to pull over my head.

The roar got louder...

...and LOUDER...

...and LOUDER!!!

The air grew as hot as an oven and the roar was awful. But then it moved on: crackle, hiss, pop, then nothing but the moan of the wind.

The mare swished her tail and nickered. Lucky for us, she hadn't blown the cork and stomped us into the ground. Slim raised up... wait, where was Slim? I found myself looking at...at a man without a head!

Well, you know me. When a headless man shows up in my foxhole, I bark! Yes sir, I fired off a couple of big ones and...okay, relax, false alarm. Ha ha. Maybe you forgot that he'd pulled his shirt over his head. Ha ha. Not me.

Okay, I'd forgotten and there for a second, he

looked exactly like some kind of headless creature, but he pulled his shirt down and he was Slim again, good old Slim, and he gave me a grin.

"It's me, Hankie, and I think we made it through the fire."

I glanced around. He was right! I flew into his arms and licked his face from ear to shining sea. Oh happy day! He wasn't a headless monster and we hadn't been turned into smoked brisket!

You know what? All my life, since I was a little guy, I had always wanted not to be smoked brisket, and here and now, my fondish wist had come true.

Slim pushed himself up to his feet and led the mare down the ravine, until he found a place where they could climb out. I followed, and once out on flat ground, we saw a huge cloud of brown smoke to the east, a solid wall that towered in the air. All around us, as far as we could see in every direction, we saw a smoking desert of black cinders.

That ocean of grass was gone, every stalk of it. Clumps of grass and yucca were still burning. Cactus pads had been baked yellow. Dried cow chips smoldered and rolled in the wind. Down along the creek, big cottonwood trees blazed away and cedar trees exploded in puffs of black smoke. And the whole world reeked of smoke. Slim looked at it for a long time and shook his head. "Man oh man, it got everything!" He looked north toward Viola's house, but couldn't see it through all the smoke. He stepped up into the saddle and pulled down his cap against the wind. "Well, we might as well find out if we have any heifers left."

He rode south, toward the spot where we'd last seen them. I noticed right away that the ground was still hot—not burn-your-feet hot but definitely warm. Yucca plants, sage brush, cedars, and mesquite trees were still burning, and we had to steer around them.

We reached the south fence and found no heifers. Most of the cedar posts had caught fire and the barbed wire had melted in several places. Slim stood up in the stirrups and looked around.

"They would have run east, away from the fire. Maybe they busted down the fence and kept going. I hope so."

We rode east a while, then Slim stopped the mare. He was staring at something up ahead. He pointed his finger, the way he does when he's counting cattle. His head sank and he mumbled, "It got 'em, every last one."

I looked to the east and saw the smoking

carcasses of ten heifers and ten baby calves. They had run as far as they could go and were bunched up against the fence when the fire swept over them.

I wanted to do or say something to make him feel better, I mean, the look on his face...

He turned the mare and we went north in a slow walk through the smoke and cinders. Slim was silent, but the wind was still screaming, filling the air with ash and the sickening smell of smoke. His face was smudged with black. The mare's hooves and ankles were black, and so were mine. We were living in a world of soot.

Up ahead, as the smoke thinned out, we saw the roof line of Viola's house, then the whole thing. It had survived, but the barn, corrals, and saddle shed were gone. Woodrow's tractor and army Jeep were blackened hulls, their tires still flaming.

Through the smoke, we saw the flashing lights of a fire truck, and men spraying water on what was left of the wooden fence around the yard. Slim's pickup had been parked in the circle drive and appeared to be okay.

We moved on toward the house. Slim stepped out of the saddle, loosened the cinch, and led the mare to the yard, the only patch of unburned grass on the place, where Woodrow had been spraying water. He dropped the reins and let her graze.

We heard a car approaching. It screeched to a stop and out stepped Chief Deputy Kile. He looked mad.

We Search
For Drover

Deputy Kile was coming our way in a fast walk, and he had a storm on his face. "What in the Sam Hill are you doing out here? I ought to throw you in jail for being so stupid!"

"Bobby, I had ten heifers and calves in that pasture, and thought I could save 'em."

"Well, that's the dumbest stunt you've pulled in a long time, and that's really saying something! I told you to get out, I told you this was a bad fire." He jabbed a finger in Slim's chest. "This thing has burned a hundred thousand acres and we're not even close to getting a handle on it. You see that tractor? That could have been YOU, and I'd have been the one to clean up your mess. Dumb! Unbelievable!"

He turned away, muttered, shook his head, and walked around in a circle. "Well, what happened?" Slim told about racing the fire and diving into the ravine. The deputy's expression didn't change. "You got lucky. God looks after fools, drunks, and cowboys, else you'd be charcoal. What about the heifers?"

Slim shook his head. "Gone. I bought 'em with borrowed money. They sure were a nice set of heifers."

The deputy's face softened. "Well, that's tough. I'm sorry. I'm afraid the death loss from this fire is going to be bad."

"How 'bout Loper and Sally May's house?"

"The Forest Service planes dropped chemical to slow down the fire. It split and went around headquarters. Last I saw, it was still there, even the corrals."

"That's good. Any idea about my place?"

The deputy removed his hat and wiped the soot and sweat off his brow with the sleeve of his shirt. "I don't know. Maybe we can drive over there, if you want to check." He looked down at me and squeezed up a tired smile, and even gave me some rubs on the head. "Hank, I'm glad you made it. Hard day, huh?" He looked at Slim. "Where's the other dog?"

Slim glanced around. "I don't know. I guess he stayed at the house."

The deputy's brows rose. "Well, let's see if we can get down the road and check."

We loaded into Deputy Kile's police car and started driving west. Trees, fence posts, and utility poles were still burning, and we had to steer around several big limbs that had fallen across the road. The pastures were black smoking deserts. We turned right at Slim's mailbox (it was still standing) and followed the dirt road to the north.

We pulled up in front of Slim's place...and it was gone, nothing but a pile of smoking rubble. I recognized the wood stove and what was left of the refrigerator. The stack of firewood on the porch was still blazing.

We got out of the car. Slim shoved his hands deep into his pockets. "Well, I won't have to wear my suit again."

He walked around the edge of the debris. Now and then, he stopped and kicked at something, then moved on. He leaned down and picked up the remains of a boot. He looked it over and tossed it away and stepped through the ashes to the refrigerator. He jerked open the door, reached inside, and brought out something black.

"My boiled turkey necks got ruined. There went supper." He left the refrigerator door hanging open and came toward us, walking with his head down. "Old Job had it right. Naked we come into this world and naked we'll leave it. A fire sure don't have much pity."

"I'm sorry, Slim."

He broke off a piece of the turkey neck and held it up to me. "You want to try some of this, pooch?"

Well, sure. I hadn't given much thought to food, but a guy should never turn down a bite of turkey neck. He pitched it in my direction and I snagged it.

Gag! It was cinderized! No thanks. I sput it out.

Slim glanced around, cupped a hand to his mouth, and called, "Drover? Come on! Here, Drover!"

We waited and watched. A minute passed. The men glanced around in a circle. Slim called again and we strained our ears, hoping...he pressed his lips together and shook his head. "He must have been on the porch when it hit. He always was a little scaredy cat."

Oh no! I couldn't believe...

We were lost in terrible thoughts when I heard a faint sound to my left. I didn't bother to look, I mean, what was there to see? Then I heard this...this voice. It said, "Oh hi. Where'd the house go?"

I whirled around and saw...you won't believe this, I guarantee you won't believe it, and you'll never guess...IT WAS DROVER! He wasn't barbecued or singed, and didn't even have a spot of soot on his coat!

He'd come through the fire without a scratch! Now, wasn't that Typical Drover? How in the world did he do it?

Slim's dirty face broke into a smile. He scooped up the little mutt and gave him a hug. "Holy cow, you made it!" He set him back on the ground and turned to Deputy Kile. "Well, I lost my heifers, my house, my clothes, everything I owned, but we've still got the dogs."

Deputy Kile chuckled. "Slim, I hate to leave you, but I've got to get back to work. They've got big problems east of here. You're welcome to stay with us. We've got plenty of room, and you can stay as long as you want."

Slim glanced around and sighed. "I don't know what comes next, Bobby, but I appreciate the offer. I'd better start checking cattle. If we've got any left alive, they won't have anything to eat."

We walked back to the car. "How much hay do you have?"

"If the hay stack didn't burn, we'll have some, but not enough for this."

"We'll get you some hay."

We drove back to Viola's place. The fire crew had put out all the fires around the house and had moved on east. Deputy Kile heard on the police radio that the fire had now grown to more than two hundred thousand acres, and the towns of Lipscomb and Higgins were being evacuated. Canadian was on high alert.

He shook his head. "This thing's liable to burn all night, maybe for days, but you're in a safe spot. There's nothing here left to burn." He offered his hand. "I'll be checking on you. If you need anything, call the sheriff's office. Keep your spirits up. Help is on the way."

He sped off to the east with his lights flashing. Slim's gaze drifted around and he took a deep breath. "Well, dogs, we've got work to do and not much daylight." On the way to headquarters, we passed thirty cows standing in the ashes. Slim slowed down and gave them a closer look. "By grabs, they made it through the fire and I can't see that they're even burned! Maybe our luck won't be all bad."

As we approached headquarters, we saw what Deputy Kile had described: the fire had split and burned on both sides of the compound, leaving everything intact: corrals, house, machine shed, stock trailers, even the hay stack.

We backed up to the stack and Slim loaded the pickup with bales. We fed the cows we had seen from the road, loaded up with more hay, and drove north to other pastures where we found the same story: blackened pastures but the cattle alive.

It was getting dark when we made it back to headquarters. Loper and Sally May hadn't returned (all the roads were still closed) and the house was empty. I figured Slim would spend the night in the house, but that wasn't his way of doing things.

We spent the night in the pickup, parked in front of the machine shed.

I was shocked and disappointed that he kicked us out of the cab and made us sleep in the back. "Y'all smell worse than a couple of roasted goats." Fine. He didn't smell so great either. But this was March and it got cold after dark, and guess who got called up for duty. Us. The dogs. When we jumped inside the cab, he said, "Y'all stink but you're warm."

He wrapped up in a couple of saddle blankets, which kind of changed the perfume in the cab (horse sweat), and we huddled up. Slim and Drover fell right off to sleep. Not me. I was worn out but couldn't sleep. Can you guess why? I had to find out how Drover had survived the fire.

I woke him up. He blinked his eyes and yawned. "Oh, hi. Where did you come from?"

"If we go back far enough, I came from my

mother."

"I'll be derned, me too. Maybe our moms were friends."

"They weren't friends."

"Yeah, after nursing nine pups, Ma wasn't very friendly."

"Our mothers weren't friends because they never met."

"I was the last pup at home. Boy, was she crabby! She locked me out of the yard and made me go look for a job."

"Drover, stop blabbering about your mother and tell me how you survived the fire."

"What fire?"

"The fire that burned the ranch and destroyed Slim's house."

"Oh, that one. Did you see it?"

"Everyone in four counties saw it. Let me refresh your memory. When Slim and I left yesterday morning, you were sitting on the porch."

"Oh yeah. Boy, what a great porch. I wonder what happened to it."

"It burned down, along with the house and half the Panhandle. How did you manage to survive?"

His eyes rolled around. "Well, let me think. I smelled smoke."

"That checks out. Go on."

"And I started hearing sounds, a crackle then a roar."

"Okay, that fits. It was the fire approaching. Go on."

"Well, you know me and loud noise. I got scared."

"Can we hurry this along? You got scared, then what?"

"Well, I ran for the machine shed."

The air hissed out of my lungs. "The machine shed was three miles away at ranch headquarters."

"Yeah, I kept looking for it and couldn't find it. And the air was hot."

"Okay, let's concentrate on that terrifying moment. The air was hot and filled with smoke, and you could hear the roar of the fire. Did you dive into a stock tank?"

"Oh no, I hate water."

"Drover, the world was in flames but you didn't even get singed. How did that happen?"

His gaze drifted around. "You know what? That moon looks just like a cantaloupe."

I stuck my nose in his face. "Stop jabbering about cantaloupes! How did you survive the fire?"

"Well, I can't remember. Wait. Maybe I fainted."

"You fainted? Okay, we're getting close to

something and this could be crucial. I need facts and details. *Where* did you faint?"

"Well, let me think here." He twisted his face into a knot. "Here we go. It must have been on the ground somewhere. I fainted on the ground. When I woke up, I couldn't find the porch, so I sat down and cried."

Why do I bother talking to the little lunatic? I wadded up the deposition and threw it in the trash.

Drover went right back to sleep, but I lay there for...snorky puffball pickle bloom zzzzzzzzzzzzzzzzzzz.

CHAPTER TEN

Help Arrives

I heard a tapping sound and my head shot up. I had been awake for hours, catching up on repeats. On reports. The sun was so bright, it almost put out my eyes, and somebody's foot was in my face, a dog's foot. Who...oh, Drover.

What was going on around here? Where was I? I blinked my eyes and glanced around.

Inside a pickup? Ah yes, the piddles of the portion began falling into puddles...into place, shall we say. The pieces of the puzzle began so forthing. We'd spent a miserable, freezing night in the pickup, and a strange man was tapping on the window. Sometimes a dog can't think of anything to say first thing in the morning, so I barked.

Okay, it was Loper. Good.

Slim roused himself out of the saddle blankets, opened the pickup door, and staggered outside. The smell of smoke hung in the air. It was cold and he hugged his arms. "I must have overslept. You got any coffee?"

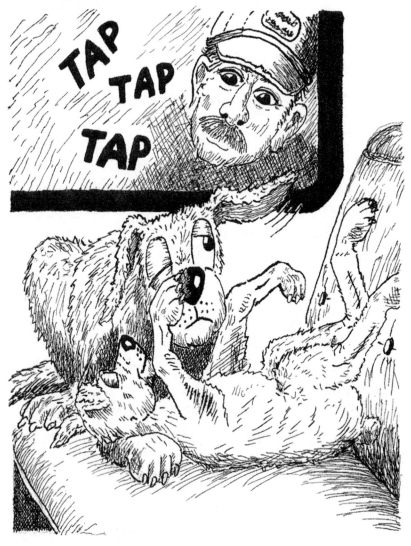

Loper handed him a thermos. "Everybody in the county has been worrying about you. How are you doing?"

"Give me a minute." He took a swig of coffee and glanced around. "I feel like a robin in a snow storm. I'm cold." Loper pitched him a warm coat. "Where'd you get that?"

"The ladies at the church sent clothes and food. I'm sorry about the house."

"Yeah, that was a shock."

"How come you slept in the pickup?"

"Well, I didn't have permission to stay in your house."

Loper rolled his eyes. "Knothead! When your house burns down...never mind, we don't have time to argue."

Loper had been listening to the news on the radio and gave Slim an update. The wildfire had burned more than three hundred thousand acres in four counties, but the wind had shifted in the night, sparing the little towns to the east of us. Even so, the damage to ranch land and livestock had been terrible.

Loper ran his eyes over the blackened landscape. "Well, do we have any cattle left?"

Slim nodded. "I fed three pastures before dark and got the full count. They weren't even burned."

"How can that be?"

"Beats me. They must have gotten in low spots and the fire blew right over 'em. I didn't find the horses."

Loper thought about that. "Well, maybe that's a good sign. If the fire had killed 'em, you would have seen something."

"That's what I figured. My heifers weren't so lucky."

Loper stared at him. "All ten? Calves too? That makes me sick."

"Me too. Let's talk about something else. What's the plan for the day?"

Loper took a deep breath and chewed his lip. "Well, we've got three hundred cows, three hundred calves, and a hundred and twenty yearlings, and they don't have one bite to eat. We have enough hay for maybe a week, and two week's worth of sacked feed. I guess we'll feed till it's gone, then...I don't know. Move the cattle? Sell out? We might be finished this time."

Slim nodded. "Don't worry about me. I'll stick around as long as I can."

"I appreciate that." Loper swiped at a tear and looked away. "We made it through the stinking drought, and now this!" We heard a roaring sound in the distance. Loper walked to the corner of the machine shed and looked east. "Do you know anything about two semi-loads of hay?"

Slim shook his head. They got into Loper's pickup and we dogs hopped into the back, and drove to the county road, where two big trucks were parked with their motors running.

The driver of the first truck, a nice red Pete, rolled down his window. "Where do you want this hay?"

"What hay? Who are you?"

"We're from Garden City, Kansas, heard about the wildfires and figured you could use some hay. We'll be back tomorrow with more."

Loper jumped on the running board and shook his hand. "Brother, you don't know how glad I am to see you! Our world is upside-down."

"Man, this place looks like the moon! I'm sure sorry about your loss."

We led the trucks to the stack lot. Instead of unloading the bales one at a time and putting them into a neat stack, Loper used the tractor to push the bales off the trailer into a big pile. That got the truckers back on the road, and Slim and Loper went to work loading both pickups with hay.

They were in the midst of doing that when three pickups pulled in, neighbors whose ranches hadn't burned. They showed up in work clothes and said, "Tell us what to do." Loper seemed a little confused at first, then said, "Load up with hay and drive until you find hungry cattle. Feed 'em, come back, load up, and do it again."

That's how the morning went, load after load of hay going out to cattle that were living in a place that looked like Death Valley, only black. What the cattle ate that day was what we threw out of the back of a pickup.

In case you wondered, I took the Lookout Position on top of every load of hay. Drover rode in the cab with Slim.

Around noon, a caravan of cars arrived from town: Sally May, Miss Viola, and some volunteers from the church. They had brought food, clothes, paper plates, blankets, jugs of drinking water, and—get this—a big sack of DOG FOOD, and it wasn't the cheap stuff we usually get around here. This was a fancy brand, Arfo, that had a rich gravy flavor.

Wow. Drover and I ate so much, we had to do Reruns on some of it. Sally May wasn't proud— that's an understatement; she was grossed out— but the men laughed. Anyway, everybody on the crew got a good hot meal, loaded up with bales, and went back to feeding the ranch.

I happened to be near Slim when he and Viola

spoke their first words since the fire. I was hoping that, well, maybe she and I could have some time alone, don't you know, but that flopped. She went straight to Slim and seemed a little, uh, raw. Angry.

"We were worried sick about you! If the sheriff hadn't called, we'd have thought you were dead! Why on earth didn't you evacuate?"

"I wanted to save our heifers."

She stared at him. "Heifers! What would I have done with heifers if you'd gotten yourself killed? You are so," she stamped her foot, "so thoughtless!"

Slim studied the ground. "Well, are you glad to see me or not?"

"Ask me later."

"We lost all ten heifers, calves too. If I'd gotten there fifteen minutes sooner, I might have been able to cut the fence and save 'em, but I was too late."

She raked him with her eyes. "We're lucky we're not at the funeral home right now, picking out your coffin!" Her eyes softened and she took a deep breath. "I'm sorry about the heifers."

"Viola, we lost eight thousand dollars and I can't pay it back. I don't even have an extra pair of socks."

"I'll get a job in town. We'll pay it off, five dollars a month for seventy years." She looked into his eyes. "Don't you get it? We still have each other, and that's *everything*. The rest is just an inconvenience."

Slim gave her a hug. "I wish I was as brave as you. I'd better get back to work."

He turned to leave and she said, "Where will you live now?"

"I don't know. I'll stay in touch. I'll be okay."

"For the record, I'm glad to see you."

He laughed. "It took you a while to say it."

And so the work began again, all afternoon: load hay, drive to a pasture, find cattle, count cattle, scatter bales of hay, back to the hay lot, and load up again. When the wind picked up in the afternoon, clouds of ash blew across the desert landscape and a few big trees along the creek burst into flames. Nobody paid attention to them because there wasn't anything left to burn. The water in the creek had turned black with ash.

Around five o'clock, we located the horses. The fence around the horse pasture had burned and fallen down, and they had drifted two miles to the northeast. They were splotched with soot but in good shape, unburned. One old mare didn't make it. She must have been too frail to outrun the fire.

Around seven, as the sun was going down, the volunteers went home and we made it back to headquarters. Slim and Loper were bushed, their faces weary and smudged with soot. A car turned at the mailbox and came our way.

It was Chief Deputy Kile. He said the wind had rekindled several fires in Hemphill County but they were mostly contained, unless the wind really cranked up and started spreading embers. Some ranchers had lost 50% of their cattle.

"I know y'all don't feel lucky, but you are. What I saw today was..." He turned to Slim. "We've still got a spare bedroom at my house."

"No thanks."

"So you're going to live in your pickup for the next year? You and the dogs?"

"Bobby, I've been busy, trying to save cattle, and haven't worked out my schedule for the year. I take life one wreck at a time, and tonight I'll sleep in my pickup. I don't want to be around people."

The deputy chuckled. "Well, son, there's a bunch of us that don't want to be around you either." Loper snorted a laugh.

"Good. Everything's working out."

The deputy flicked some ash off his uniform. "There's a camper trailer parked where your house used to be."

"What?"

"I got a call from a man in Amarillo. He'd heard about the fire and asked what he could do to help. I said, 'I know this cowboy. He's crabby, nobody can get along with him, and he's not very smart, but he needs a place to stay.' The gentleman brought a camper trailer and people showed up to help. Electricity's out, so Scot and J.B. hooked it up to a generator. Bennie and Jake came over from Gruver and got the water running."

"Bobby, I'm kind of tired. Is this one of your jokes?"

"Nope. A lot of people are thinking about you. It's a cute little trailer, twice as good as you deserve." He pitched Slim a set of keys. "Porch light's on and it's got a little shower." He turned to Loper. "You can use it as long as you need it."

Loper was shocked. "Who is this guy?"

"I don't even know his name, somebody who wanted to help. If y'all need anything, let me know."

He got into his car and drove off. Loper shook his head. "Well, that beats it all. Just when you think the world's got no heart, everybody shows up to help."

Slim nodded. "It makes it hard to keep up a

bad attitude." He yawned. "Man alive, this ranch is a work horse."

"Yeah, and sometimes I wonder if it's worth it."

Slim gave him a tired look. "It's worth it."

"We've got plenty of food at the house."

"No thanks. Shower'll do me. I'm tired, and tired of smelling smoke. See you in the morning."

CHAPTER ELEVEN

The Mysterious Marsh Berries

We loaded into the pickup and headed for what used to be Slim's shack. It was almost dark now and we could see little fires burning along the creek.

Drover was riding in the middle, of course, because he hadn't been certified for the Shotgun Position. It's an important job and you don't get it just because you want it. We have a training program and you have to pass a test. Drover had flunked it ten times in a row, a perfect record.

That's why we put him in the middle of the seat, where he could do the least amount of damage.

Anyway, the fires along the creek looked a little creepy and he got creeped out. "Oh my gosh, look at those campfires!"

"Those are big trees that are still smoldering."

"Yeah, but they look like campfires."

"They're not campfires."

"Yeah, but what if they are, and what if... what if it's the Charlies!"

Hm, I hadn't thought of that. I took a closer look. "You know, they do look like campfires, now that you mention it."

"See? I told you."

"Please don't gloat. Why would the Charlies be camping out after a prairie fire?"

"Well, maybe they wanted to marsh some roastmallows."

"Do you mean 'roast some marshmallows'?"

"Yeah, that's what I said."

"That's *not* what you said."

"What did I say?"

"You said they're roasting marsh berries."

"Gosh, do we have marsh berries around here?"

"I don't know. Maybe we have a few, yes. You'd find them along the edges of the creek. Marsh berries grow in marshes, don't you see. Marshes are wet and creeks are wet."

"I'll be derned. I wonder why."

"They're wet because they contain water."

"Oh yeah, and water's wet too."

"Exactly my point. It all fits together: wet

water, wet creek, and wet marsh, and that's where you find marsh berries."

"And the Charlies eat 'em?"

"I suppose they do, yes. What else could they find to eat in March?"

"I'll be derned. So they're eating roasted March marsh berries?"

"You could put it that way, I guess."

An odd gleam came to his eyes and he sat up in the seat. "I just got an idea for song. You want to hear it?"

"You know, we're kind of busy right now."

"Listen to this." He sat up tall in the seat and let 'er rip.

> March marsh berries march, roasting by
> the stream.
> Merrily, merrily, marsh and mellowly, pass
> the bowl of cream.

He gave me a grin. "What do you think?"

"It makes no sense."

"Yeah, but it rhymed and everything."

"Okay, it rhymed. So what?"

"Well, I wrote it myself, hee hee, and we could do it as a round."

"A round what?"

"A round song. I'll start it off and you come in. It'll be great."

This was *so silly*, but what could I do? I was trapped inside a pickup with the little goof. "All right, let's get it over with."

So we sang it as a round. He was so proud of it, we had to do it several times. When we got done, he was almost beside himself. "That's the coolest song I ever wrote!"

"Drover, it was a little jingle about marsh berries, but not even close to being serious music."

His smile faded. "Wait a second. Did you say 'marsh berries'?"

"Of course I did. That's what your song was about."

"Yeah, but I meant *marshmallows*. I've never heard of marsh berries."

My vision went red. "Look, pal, we've already had this discussion, and you were the one who brought it up."

"I thought you did."

"I had never heard of stupid marsh berries until you started blabbering and sang a pathetic little song about them!"

His face crumbled. "You didn't like my song?"

"Are you kidding? That was one of the..." I stared out the window and tried to calm myself.

The captain of the ship must never lose his compost. His compossum. His composure. I took several deep breaths. "Drover, it disturbs me that we're discussing something that neither of us has ever heard of. Does that strike you as weird?"

His head began to sink. "Yeah, I worry about myself sometimes."

"So do I. Is there something you need to tell me about marshmallows? Have you ever wanted to be one?"

"I don't think so."

"That's good. Let's not tell anyone about this conversation. It wouldn't do the Security Division any good."

"Yeah, it might sound like two dumb dogs talking."

"Exactly. It could damage the morale of this unit. As far as the outside world is concerned, we've never discussed marshmallows or marsh berries."

"Yeah, and we don't believe in marsh berries anyway, so there!" He stuck out his tongue at something, I don't know what. "What did you think of my song? Be honest."

"Great song. I'm speechless."

He squeezed up a grin. "Gosh, thanks. I feel better now. Thanks a lot."

"Glad to do it, son. That's what I'm here for."

My brains were scrambled. He does this to me all the time, you know, lures me into loony conversations that go around in circles and make me wonder if I'm going insane.

Why would two ranch dogs be singing and

talking about...never mind, let's just drop it.

We made it to Slim's place around sundown, and it was a sad spectacle that greeted us: a pile of ash and debris where Drover and I had spent many pleasant nights in front of the stove, and where Drover had spent many nights barfing and wetting on the floor. Those stains were gone now and Slim would never know the truth about Drover's nighttime adventures.

But then we saw a shiny silver tube parked nearby, the camper trailer Deputy Kile had talked about. The generator was humming, the porch light was on, and it looked pretty inviting. Slim looked it over and reached for the door handle. I was right there, ready to...

"Where do you think you're going?"

Well, I...inside, of course. I mean, that's where dogs belong. What's a camper without a dog to camp with? It would be like a house without a home.

I went to Slow Wags on the tail section and beamed him a look that said, "Our house burned down. We've lost our porch. We're homeless dogs, tired and hungry, weary, sad, and discouraged, looking for one true friend in this cold, uncaring world."

I studied his face and saw ice. "Hank, you're

filthy. You look like you've been rolling around in a fireplace." He went inside and slammed the door.

Oh brother. How's a dog supposed to look when his world burns down? Oh well. I knew he would change his mind. One hour alone in the trailer would soften his heart and he would BEG me to come inside. I could wait.

I found a spot near the door of the trailer, flopped down, ignored Drover, and waited for Slim to call me into the house.

Perhaps I fell into a light doze. Then...I heard a mysterious sound and leaped to my feet. I was outside, in front of a silver space vehicle, and, good grief, some kind of creature was coming down the ladder!

Okay, the Charlies had been roasting marsh berries around campfires, and now they had landed in the yard! I went straight into Code Red and fired off several blasts of Stage One Barking.

"Will you dry up?"

Huh?

Wait, hold up. Ha ha. It was morning and Slim was coming out of the camper trailer. See? I had brought the ranch through another dangerous night, but that camper really did look like a space ship, no kidding.

He was wearing clothes, Slim was, the same

jeans and shirt he'd been wearing the day before, because they were the only rags he had left after the fire, and they were almost black with soot.

He had washed the soot off his face and run a rake through his hair. I went to him and gave him Broad Swings on the tail section, delivering the message, "Pretty sad night without your dogs, I guess."

He grumbled something and walked past me to the ruins of his former house. Naturally, I went with him, I mean, we hadn't confronted the Breakfast Situation yet and I wanted to stack up a few points.

He found the rusted gun barrel of what used to be his .22 rifle and stirred the ashes around. Hm. Maybe he was looking for the puddle Drover had left under his bed.

He reached down and lifted something out of the ashes. One of his spurs. He stirred some more ash and found the other one. The leather straps were gone, but at least he'd found the spurs, and he seemed pleased. "Well, I ain't completely wiped out."

Just then, we heard the sound of an approaching vehicle. I was about to Launch All Dogs when I saw Viola's daddy's pickup, and she was driving. She parked in front of the camper and got out. She wore a pretty yellow dress and waved and, my goodness, the whole world just sparkled with her smile. It was as though someone had opened the drapes in a dungeon.

I ran to her and she said, "Morning, Hank!" Wow! She let down the tailgate and brought out two lawn chairs and set them up in front of the camper, just as Slim arrived. "How was the camper?"

"Pretty nice. It sure beats a cardboard box."

"Have you had breakfast?"

"No, I'm a little short on groceries."

"Here's breakfast." She pointed to a thermos of coffee, and pans that held scrambled eggs, bacon, sausage, and homemade biscuits, and a jar of wild plum jelly.

Slim's mouth dropped open. "Good honk, you went to a lot of trouble."

She gave him a cute smile. "A little. Mom made the biscuits. Help yourself."

He poured himself a cup of coffee, filled a paper plate with grub, and plopped down in one of the chairs. Naturally, I...

"Buzz off, Shep."

Naturally, I kept a respectful distance and observed. I mean, our people don't always appreciate dogs drooling at them at breakfast time.

What a grouch.

CHAPTER TWELVE

Together In This

Viola brought her plate and joined him. "Well, how are you feeling today?"

"You ever seen an ant den after a road grader plowed over it? The ants walk around in circles all day. That's how I feel. That old house wasn't much, but I'm going to miss it. And I lost my saddle."

She took a bite of scrambled eggs. "You wouldn't believe how people have responded to this fire. Our phone has been ringing off the wall: 'What can we do to help? What does Slim need?' They're driving out from town with food, groceries, clothes, kitchen items. They can't find you, so they're leaving it with me and Sally May. I have three boxes of things in the pickup."

"Good honk. I'm surprised they even knew about it."

"Well, since you're a hermit, you don't know that it was one of the biggest fires in Texas history. It's been in the newspapers and on the radio, and help is coming from all over the country: hay, sacked feed, vet supplies, fencing material. There's a line of trucks in Twitchell, waiting to unload."

"I'll be." He poked at his food. "I don't suppose you've heard from the banker."

"Yes. He called and wanted to talk to you."

"Oh good."

"I explained that your phone is a lump of melted plastic, and that you're working daylight to dark, trying to keep cattle alive."

"I don't reckon he cried, did he?"

"No."

"Did he say anything about debtor's prison?"

"Not that I recall."

"Well, what did he say?"

"He said," she gestured in the air with her fork, "that the cattle note is on hold and won't draw any interest until things straighten out."

He stared at her. "I'll be derned. But things won't straighten out, Viola. Those heifers are gone. We didn't even get a package of hamburger

107

out of 'em and we still owe eight thousand dollars."

"The Lord takes care of every sparrow."

"Birds don't borrow money."

"We'll get through it."

We heard a vehicle approaching. Slim and Viola looked toward the sound and somehow Slim's sausage...well, it disappeared. It was very slurp...very mysterious.

Loper's flatbed pickup pulled into view. He got out and walked toward us, wearing his usual Morning Face. Glum. He glanced at the pans of food in the bed of Viola's pickup. "You've fallen into luxury since I saw you last."

"It ain't a bad life. Help yourself."

Loper grabbed a biscuit and smeared it with wild plum jelly. "Where do you want those heifers?"

"What heifers?"

"All day yesterday and into the night, people were calling to donate a heifer. George Clay's running the deal and he's holding ten head in his pens. He wants to know where to haul 'em."

"You're kidding me." Slim shot a glance at Viola. She shrugged and gave him an innocent smile. "I don't have a place for heifers."

Viola said, "Of course you do. Daddy's letting us use his pasture."

"Yeah, but it's burned down to the dirt, and we don't have any hay."

She seemed surprised. "Really? When I left the house, two nice men from Garden City were unloading a truckload of alfalfa. If that's not enough, I've got a list of ten people who want to donate more. We could probably have five thousand bales here by tomorrow night."

Slim seemed bewildered. "I don't deserve this."

Loper took a snap off his biscuit. "I agree, but what can you do? I'll tell George to unload the heifers at Woodrow's pens."

"Woodrow ain't got any pens. They burned to the ground."

"George's hired man is bringing portable panels and he'll set up a pen. They're eight to nine months pregnant and George didn't offer to calve 'em out. You'll have to do that yourself." He wiped his hands on his jeans. "Well, are you going to eat all day or can we squeeze in a few hours' work?"

Slim chuckled and shook his head. "Loper, it ain't even eight o'clock yet."

"When you get burned out, the days start early. I'll see you at the hay lot, if you can work it into your schedule." He waved a farewell and drove off.

Slim shook his head. "Don't he beat it all?" He looked into his plate. "Hey, where'd my sausage go?" His eyes came at me like arrows. "Hank!"

Sausage? What burp sausage? Excuse me. I knew almost nothing about his sausage, but I had a suspect: Drover! Where was the little thief?

Viola said, "Do you want to see what's in the boxes?"

They went to her pickup. The first box contained secondhand clothes: five pairs of faded jeans and six long-sleeved shirts. Out of the second box he pulled an insulated vest, socks, boxer shorts, T-shirts, and a wool cap. In the third box he found a cooking pot, two plates, a coffee mug, spoons, forks, knives, and a can opener.

"Sally May is putting together a box of groceries."

"Tell her I need a can of coffee, fifty cans of mackerel, and ten pounds of frozen turkey necks. She can feed the rest to the dogs."

Viola rolled her eyes. "Bachelors."

He found an envelope with no writing on it. He opened it and pulled out six fifty-dollar bills.

"What's this?"

"It looks like cash."

"Who's it from?"

"Santa Claus, I guess."

"Not Woodrow."

"Maybe."

"He doesn't even like me."

"You exaggerate. With Daddy, it's hard to tell sometimes."

"I'm not used to taking charity."

She parked her hands on her hips. "Well, mister, you'd better practice up. They've started a fund at the bank and checks are coming in from all over the place. In the Texas Panhandle, if you don't want charity, don't let your house burn down."

He shook his head and gazed off into the distance. "I don't know what to say."

She went to the pickup and brought out a cassette tape player. "I want you to listen to a song by an Amarillo group, Comanche Moon."

"Viola, I really ought to..."

"Shhh. Your boss and the cattle can wait. Sit down and listen."

They sat down and she started the tape.

Together In This

When you come back home to a burned
  out house
You're shuffling through the ashes, feeling
  broke and turned out;
When you don't know where you're gonna go
  when the night comes
You've got your friends and your family
  standing by your side.

And we'll be the ones you hold onto, the ones
  you know are always there.
We'll be the melody you're humming that
  goes, "I am not alone, we're gonna be
  together in this."

When you're growing old and the lights are
  getting dim
And you have to go to funerals just to see a
  friend
Feels like you're tilting at windmills every
  time you open your mouth
Well it's not too late to dream a dream for
  what you love; it's not too late to find
  someone who'll be there when you need it,

Someone that you can hold onto, someone
  you know is always there;
Who'll be the melody you're humming that
  goes, "I am not alone, we're gonna be
  together in this."

People say that we die alone, but we don't
  have to live that way
'Cause in the soul of everyone is the need to
  believe and to give.

So when you're sitting at your table with the
  ones that you love
Remember the ones who've gone before you
  and the ones who are alone
Try to give a hand to one who needs it, say a
  word for one who cannot speak
Give a thought for the ones who are forgotten.
  Doesn't matter if they're living right, don't
  wait for them to reach out if they need

Someone that they can hold onto, someone
  they know is always there;
You can be the melody they're humming that
  goes, "I am not alone, we're gonna be
  together in this."

Viola shut off the tape and they sat in silence for a while. Slim said, "That's mighty fine. Where'd you run into it?"

"They were playing it on the radio yesterday morning as a tribute to all the fire victims. I thought it said a lot. *We're together in this.*"

"Thanks for playing it. And thanks for the breakfast too."

She laid a hand on his shoulder. "Slim, in all of Texas history, there has never been a report of a banker eating a cowboy. Try to remember that."

He smiled. "That'll get me through the day." He stood there for a minute, moving his feet around, then swooped down and gave her a kiss on the cheek. "Thanks again. Come on, dogs!"

Slim and I loaded into his pickup. Drover was a no-show until he heard the pickup door slam, and here he came like a little bottle rocket. Slim let him in and he took his spot in the middle of the seat.

He said, "I sure didn't want to get left. Last time I stayed at the house, it burned down."

And so we launched ourselves into another day of Life After the Fire: loading hay, feeding cattle, clearing rubble, and repairing miles of burned fence. People showed up to help and brought food, clothes, and more hay. Slim and

Viola got their heifers back, donated by ten nice people who didn't give their names, and all of us started life all over again.

I guess that's about the end...wait, we have one more detail. The day after the fire, Sally May still couldn't find her cat. She looked everywhere and walked out into the pasture, calling his name. Night came and no cat.

The next day, I was supervising the men

whilst they loaded hay, and who do you suppose showed up like flies at a picnic? The cat. Pete. He came sliding down the north side of the pickup, rubbing the tires, purring like a little chainsaw, and smirking, of course. Always smirking, that's the cat.

In his annoying whiny voice, he said, "Well, well, it's Hankie the Wonderdog! How was your fire?"

Was I glad to see the little pestilence? Let's be honest. I felt a tiny particle of gladness, but you don't need to blab it around. Let's just say that I had mixed feelings, and leave it there.

We all survived the fire, is the point, and this case is closed.

The Real Fire

FIRE ON THE MCROSS RANCH

FEEDING CATTLE AFTER THE FIRE

On March 6, 2017, John and Kris Erickson and family lost their home and ranch to the third largest wildfire in Texas history.

In the days that followed, the outpouring of prayers, love, and support that they received from friends, family, Hank the Cowdog fans, teachers, librarians, and young children from around the country took their breath away.

Boxes of mail arrived from friends they'd never met, expressing sympathy for their loss and their appreciation for the joy that the Hank books had brought into their lives. Moreoever, friends and neighbors rallied around them with food, help, and encouragement.

SPURS SALVAGED FROM THE RUBBLE

That love, shown in so many ways, was a tremendous source of encouragement during a sad time.

NOCONA, ONE OF THE MCROSS HORSES, AFTER THE FIRE

JOHN R. ERICKSON SIGNING COPIES OF HANK #69 TO GIVE AS A "THANK YOU" TO VOLUNTEERS WHO HELPED CLEAR AWAY THE RUBBLE OF THE HOUSE

Dear friends,

We're already embarking on the road to rebuilding.

Thank you, Hank readers and friends, for your letters, prayers, and help!

You have been an incredible blessing to us!

- John and Kris Erickson

SOME OF THE LETTERS AND CARDS SENT BY FRIENDS AND HANK READERS AROUND THE COUNTRY IN THE DAYS IMMEDIATELY AFTER THE FIRE

BONSMARA CATTLE ON THE BURNED GROUND

Miss Viola's Homemade Biscuits

Ingredients:

- 2 & 1/2 cups flour
- 1 tablespoon baking powder
- 1 teaspoon salt
- 1/2 cup salted butter
- 1 cup cheddar cheese
- 1 tablespoon chives
- 3 tablespoons honey
- 1 cup milk

Instructions:

1. Preheat the oven to 425°F.
2. In a mixing bowl, stir together the flour, baking powder and salt.
3. Next, using a pastry-blender, cut the butter into the mixture.
4. Add the cheese and chives and stir.
5. Stir-in the honey and milk to form a soft dough.
6. Place the dough on a floured surface and coat with a little flour.
7. Knead dough a little by turning and folding it over itself about 5 or 6 times until less sticky.
8. Roll dough to desired thickness and cut into rounds with a biscuit cutter or the top of a drinking glass.
9. Arrange biscuits on a parchment-paper covered cookie sheet with sides touching, and bake until golden brown on top (about 12-13 minutes).

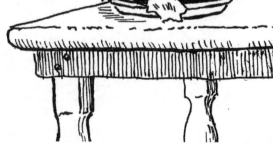

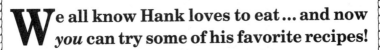

We all know Hank loves to eat... and now *you* can try some of his favorite recipes!

Have you visited
Sally May's Kitchen yet?
http://www.hankthecowdog.com/recipes

Here, you'll find recipes for:

Sally May's Apple Pie
Hank's Picante Sauce
Round-Up Green Beans
Little Alfred's and Baby Molly's Favorite Cookies
Cowboy Hamburgers with Gravy
Chicken-Ham Casserole
...and MORE!

Have you read all of Hank's adventures?

Join Hank the Cowdog's Security Force

Are you a big Hank the Cowdog fan? Then you'll want to join Hank's Security Force. Here is some of the neat stuff you will receive:

Welcome Package
- A Hank paperback of your choice
- An original Hank poster (19" x 25")
- A Hank bookmark

Eight digital issues of *The Hank Times* newspaper with
- Lots of great games and puzzles
- Stories about Hank and his friends
- Special previews of future books
- Fun contests

More Security Force Benefits
- Special discounts on Hank books, audios, and more
- Special Members Only section on Hank's website at www.hankthecowdog.com

Total value of the Welcome Package and *The Hank Times* is $23.99. However, your two-year membership is **only $7.99** plus $5.00 for shipping and handling.

☐ Yes, I want to join Hank's Security Force. Enclosed is $12.99 ($7.99 + $5.00 for shipping and handling) for my **two-year membership**. [Make check payable to Maverick Books. International shipping extra.]

WHICH BOOK WOULD YOU LIKE TO RECEIVE IN YOUR WELCOME PACKAGE? CHOOSE ANY BOOK IN THE SERIES. (EXCEPT #50)   (#   )

	BOY or GIRL
YOUR NAME	(CIRCLE ONE)

MAILING ADDRESS

CITY	STATE	ZIP

TELEPHONE	BIRTH DATE

E-MAIL   (REQUIRED FOR DIGITAL HANK TIMES)

Send check or money order for $12.99 to:

Hank's Security Force
Maverick Books
P.O. Box 549
Perryton, Texas 79070
Offer is subject to change

DO NOT SEND CASH.   NO CREDIT CARDS ACCEPTED.
ALLOW 2-3 WEEKS FOR DELIVERY

The following activities are samples from *The Hank Times*, the official newspaper of Hank's Security Force. Please do not write on these pages unless this is your book. And, even then, why not just find a scrap of paper?

"Rhyme Time"

W hat if Miss Viola's father, Woodrow, decides to give up ranching and go in search of other jobs? What kinds of jobs could he find?

Make a rhyme using "Woodrow" that would relate to his new job possibilities.

Example: Woodrow starts a business that makes arrow-shooters.
Answer: Woodrow BOW

1. Woodrow becomes a school crosswalk person telling kids when to cross.

2. Woodrow opens a pet shop selling turtles and snails.

3. Woodrow starts a lawn care business.

4. Woodrow gets his own TV program.

5. Woodrow helps people find their seats at concerts.

6. Woodrow opens a balloon store for special occasions.

7. Woodrow measures people's height at doctor's appointments.

8. Woodrow starts a shirt repair business.

Answers:

1. Woodrow GO
2. Woodrow SLOW
3. Woodrow MOW
4. Woodrow SHOW
5. Woodrow ROW
6. Woodrow BLOW
7. Woodrow GROW
8. Woodrow SEW

"Photogenic" Memory Quiz

We all know that Hank has a "photogenic" memory—being aware of your surroundings is an important quality for a Head of Ranch Security. Now *you* can test your powers of observation.

How good is your memory? Look at the illustration on the cover and try to remember as many things about it as possible. Then turn back to this page and see how many questions you can answer.

1. How many rabbits were there? 0, 1, 2, or 3?

2. What color was Slim's shirt? Blue, Gray, Orange, or Red?

3. Was Hank looking to *his* left or right?

4. What color was Slim's hat? Blue, Gray, Orange, or Red?

5. Could you see Drover's tail?

6. How many of Slim's hands could you see? 0, 1, 2, or all 3?

"Word Maker"

Try making up to twenty words from the letters in the names below. Use as many letters as possible, however, don't just add an "s" to a word you've already listed in order to have it count as another. Try to make up entirely new words for each line!

Then, count the total number of letters used in all of the words you made, and see how well you did using the Security Force Rankings below!

WOODROW   KILE

_____	_____
_____	_____
_____	_____
_____	_____
_____	_____
_____	_____
_____	_____
_____	_____
_____	_____
_____	_____

59-61 You spend too much time with J.T. Cluck and the chickens.

62-64 You are showing some real Security Force potential.

65-68 You have earned a spot on our Ranch Security team.

69+   Wow! You rank up there as a top-of-the-line cowdog.

Have you visited Hank's official website yet?

www.hankthecowdog.com

Don't miss out on exciting *Hank the Cowdog* games and activities, as well as up-to-date news about upcoming books in the series!

When you visit, you'll find:

- Hank's BLOG, which is the first place we announce upcoming books and new products!
- Hank's Official Shop, with tons of great *Hank the Cowdog* books, audiobooks, games, t-shirts, stuffed animals, mugs, bags, and more!
- Links to Hank's social media, whereby Hank sends out his "Cowdog Wisdom" to fans.
- A FREE, printable "Map of Hank's Ranch"!
- Hank's Music Page where you can listen to songs and even download FREE ringtones!
- A way to sign up for Hank's free email updates
- Sally May's "Ranch Roundup Recipes"!
- Printable & Colorable Greeting Cards for Holidays.

- Articles about Hank and author John R. Erickson in the news,

...AND MUCH, MUCH MORE!

search the website | GO

BOOKS
The Collection

FAN ZONE
Fun & Games

AUTHOR
Meet the Creator

STORE
Books & More

Find Toys, Games, Books & More
at the Hank shop.

ANNOUNCING:
A sneak peek at Hank #66

Ever thought of having a Hank the Cowdog themed party?

Hank Plays Cupid:

GAMES
COME PLAY WITH HANK & PALS

BOOKS
BROWSE THE ENTIRE HANK CATALOG

FRIENDS
GET TO KNOW THE RANCH GANG

 Visit Hank's Facebook page

 Follow Hank on Twitter

 Watch Hank on YouTube

 Follow Hank on Pinterest

 Send Hank an Email

FROM THE BLOG

JAN 28 Hank is Cupid in Disguise...

JAN 18 The Valentine's Day Robbery! - a Snippet from the Story

DEC 04 Getting SIGNED Hank the Cowdog books for Christmas!

OCT 14 Education Association's lists of recommended books?

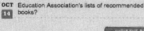 VISIT THE BLOG

Hank's Survey
We'd love to know what you think! | GO

TEACHER'S CORNER

Download fun activity guides, discussion questions and more.

SALLY MAY'S RECIPES

 Discover delicious recipes from Sally May herself. | GO

Hank's Music
Free ringtones, music and more!

 MORE

Official Shop
Find books, audio, toys and more!

 LET'S GO

Join Hank's Security Force
Get the activity letter and other cool stuff.

 JOIN | SECURITY FORCE

Get the Latest

Keep up with Hank's news and promotions by signing up for our e-news.

Looking for The Hank Times fan club newsletter?

 Enter your email address | SIGN UP

Hank in the News

Find out what the media is saying about Hank. | GO

FEATURED BOOK

The Christmas Turkey Disaster

Now Available!

Hank is in real trouble this time. L...

BUY | READ | LISTEN

BOOKS
Browse Titles
Buy Books
Audio Samples
Other Books

FAN ZONE
Games
Hank & Friends
Security Force
Educational Stuff

AUTHOR
John Erickson's Bio
Hank in the News
In Concert
Contact John

SHOP
The Books
Store
Get Help
Retailer Info

And, be sure to check out the
Audiobooks!

If you've never heard a *Hank the Cowdog* audiobook, you're missing out on a lot of fun! Each Hank book has also been recorded as an unabridged audiobook for the whole family to enjoy!

Praise for the Hank Audiobooks:

"It's about time the Lone Star State stopped hogging Hank the Cowdog, the hilarious adventure series about a crime solving ranch dog. Ostensibly for children, the audio renditions by author John R. Erickson are sure to build a cult following among adults as well." — *Parade Magazine*

"Full of regional humor . . . vocals are suitably poignant and ridiculous. A wonderful yarn." — *Booklist*

"For the detectin' and protectin' exploits of the canine Mike Hammer, hang Hank's name right up there with those of other anthropomorphic greats...But there's no sentimentality in Hank: he's just plain more rip-roaring fun than the others. Hank's misadventures as head of ranch security on a spread somewhere in the Texas Panhandle are marvelous situation comedy." — *School Library Journal*

"Knee-slapping funny and gets kids reading."

— *Fort Worth Star Telegram*

Teacher's Corner

Know a teacher who uses Hank in their classroom? You'll want to be sure they know about Hank's "Teacher's Corner"! Just click on the link on the homepage, and you'll find free teacher's aids, such as a printable map of Hank's ranch, a reading log, coloring pages, blog posts specifically for teachers and librarians, and much more!

Love Hank's Hilarious Songs?

Hank the Cowdog's "Greatest Hits" albums bring together the music from the unabridged audiobooks you know and love! These wonderful collections of hilarious (and sometimes touching) songs are unmatched. Where else can you learn about coyote philosophy, buzzard lore, why your dog is protecting an old corncob, how bugs compare to hot dog buns, and much more!

And, be sure to visit Hank's "Music Page" on the official website to listen to some of the songs and download FREE Hank the Cowdog ringtones!

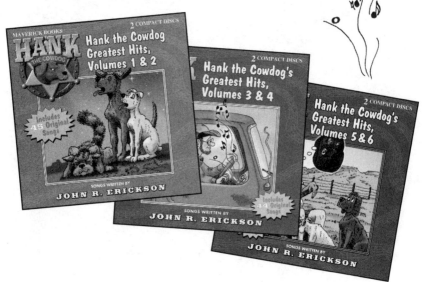

"Audio-Only" Stories

Ever wondered what those "Audio-Only" Stories in Hank's Official Store are all about?

The Audio-Only Stories are Hank the Cowdog adventures that have never been released as books. They are about half the length of a typical Hank book, and there are currently seven of them. They have run as serial stories in newspapers for years and are now available as audiobooks!

John R. Erickson,

a former cowboy, has written numerous books for both children and adults and is best known for his acclaimed *Hank the Cowdog* series. The *Hank* series began as a self-publishing venture in Erickson's garage in 1982 and has endured to become one of the nation's most popular series for children and families.

Through the eyes of Hank the Cowdog, a smelly, smart-aleck Head of Ranch Security, Erickson gives readers a glimpse into daily life on a cattle ranch in the West Texas Panhandle. His stories have won a number of awards, including the Audie, Oppenheimer, Wrangler, and Lamplighter Awards, and have been translated into Spanish, Danish, Farsi, and Chinese. *USA Today* calls the *Hank the Cowdog* books "the best family entertainment in years." Erickson lives and works on his ranch in Perryton, Texas, with his family.

Gerald L. Holmes

is a largely self-taught artist who grew up on a ranch in Oklahoma. For over thirty-five years, he has illustrated the *Hank the Cowdog* books and serial stories, as well as numerous other cartoons and textbooks, and his paintings have been featured in various galleries across the United States. He and his wife live in Perryton, Texas, where they raised their family, and where he continues to paint his wonderfully funny and accurate portrayals of modern American ranch life to this day.